"What is it?" Adam demanded,
his low voice rough to Emma's ears.

"Why do you shy away from contact with me
as if I'll contaminate you in some way? Is it men
in general? Were you attacked and it's left you
frightened of the rest of us? Or—" a sudden
thought struck him and he blinked "—do you
prefer women to men?"

"No." Emma shook her head in violent repudiation.
"It's nothing like that." She realized that, far from
being straightened out, the situation was growing
more complicated by the minute.

"It's everybody." The words finally escaped her
precarious control. "It's not just you...I can't
touch anybody...."

Dear Reader,

Perhaps you are driving home one evening when you spot a rotating flashing light or hear a siren. Instantly, your pulse quickens—it's human nature. You can't help responding to these signals that there is an emergency somewhere close by.

Heartbeat, romances being published in North America for the first time, brings you the fast-paced kinds of stories that trigger responses to life-and-death situations. The heroes and heroines whose lives you will share in this exciting series of books devote themselves to helping others, to saving lives, to *caring.* And while they are devotedly doing what they do best, they manage to fall in love!

Since these books are largely set in the U.K., Australia and New Zealand, and mainly written by authors who reside in those countries, the medical terms originally used may be unfamiliar to North American readers. Because we wanted to ensure that you enjoyed these stories as thoroughly as possible, we've taken a few special measures. Within the stories themselves, we have substituted American terms for British ones we felt would be very unfamiliar to you. And we've also included in these books a short glossary of terms that we've left in the stories, so as not to disturb their authenticity, but that you might wonder about.

So prepare to feel your heart beat a little faster! You're about to experience love when life is on the line!

Yours sincerely,

Marsha Zinberg,
Executive Editor, Harlequin Books

LOUD AND CLEAR

Josie Metcalfe

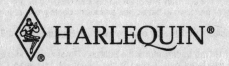

HARLEQUIN®

TORONTO • NEW YORK • LONDON
AMSTERDAM • PARIS • SYDNEY • HAMBURG
STOCKHOLM • ATHENS • TOKYO • MILAN • MADRID
PRAGUE • WARSAW • BUDAPEST • AUCKLAND

ISBN 0-373-51274-0

LOUD AND CLEAR

First North American Publication 2003

Copyright © 1996 by Josie Metcalfe

Josie Metcalfe lives in Cornwall now with her long-suffering husband, four children and two horses, but as an army brat frequently on the move, books were the only friends that came with her wherever she went. Now that she writes them herself, she is constantly making new friends and hates saying goodbye at the end of a book—but there are always more characters in her head clamoring for attention until she can't wait to tell their stories.

GLOSSARY

A and E—accident and emergency department

B and G—bloods and glucose

Consultant—an experienced specialist registrar who is the leader of a medical team; there can be a junior and senior consultant on a team

CVA—cerebrovascular accident

Duty registrar—the doctor on call

FBC—full blood count

Fixator—an external device, similar to a frame, for rigidly holding bones together while they heal

GA—general anesthetic

GCS—the Glasgow Coma Scale, used to determine a patient's level of consciousness

Houseman/house officer—British equivalent of a medical intern or clerk

MI—myocardial infarction

Obs—observations re: pulse, blood pressure, etc.

Registrar/specialist registrar—a doctor who is trained in a particular area of medicine

Resus—room or unit where a patient is taken for resuscitation after cardiac accident

Rostered—scheduled

Rota—rotation

RTA—road traffic accident

Senior House Officer (SHO)—British equivalent of a resident

Theatre—operating room

CHAPTER ONE

'No!'

She sat up in the darkness, the bedclothes tangled around her waist and legs. Her pulse was racing and her breathing was wildly erratic.

'Not again!' she moaned, pressing her hands against her temples as if she could remove with brute force the visions which filled her head.

She had fought so hard to stop this happening and for nearly two years she had believed that she had conquered it.

Now this!

She shivered as the sweat cooled on her skin, her cotton nightdress clammy against her breasts and over the discouraged slump of her spine.

As her pulse began to slow, the vivid details of the nightmare gradually faded until all she was left with was an after-image of torment.

To herself, she'd often compared it to the image she could see after she'd looked at something too bright, almost as if it were seared on the retina of the eye— only in her case it was burned into her mind.

Someone out there had managed to break through the shield that she had erected between herself and the rest of the world. Someone had made a mental connection, letting her experience their tearing anguish at first hand.

Who was it? Whose pain had she—?

No! She didn't want to know. That part of her life was over.

She shivered again as she glanced across at the numbers on her alarm. Still an hour before she needed to get up for work but there was no point in trying to go back to sleep now. She closed her eyes and shook her head despondently as the misery overtook her once more and her shoulders drooped.

She couldn't bear it if it all started again. This time it had been stronger than ever. Please God, it would be someone just passing through the area, she thought. Perhaps when they went back to wherever they came from they would take their dreadful suffering away with them.

The alternative was too awful to consider. She had spent too long and worked too hard to overcome it last time to contemplate having everything destroyed again.

Her lingering fear was like a small dark cloud in the corner of her mind when she arrived at the hospital.

'Hello, Em,' Charge Nurse Dave Maddox called. 'I hope you had a good rest yesterday because it looks like it's going to be bedlam here. It's a fine, sunny, bank-holiday weekend and the traffic on the motorway is already building up nicely. It won't be long before some lunatic causes mayhem just to keep us on our toes.'

'Thanks!' Emma pulled a face at him and he grinned in reply before continuing through the department towards the ringing phone.

Emma made for the staffroom to leave her jacket and handbag, knowing that she'd arrived in plenty of time to change into her uniform.

A quick trip to the bathroom to check that her rebellious hair was all tucked neatly under her cap showed her a disturbing glimpse of her reflection and she leant towards the mirror, frowning at the dark circles showing through the pale skin under her silvery grey eyes. If it hadn't been for her thick dark eyelashes she would have been in danger of looking like a panda.

She smoothed a hand over the curl which had escaped, and subdued it with an extra pin, added to the armoury already holding the confining twist of hair, before she finally turned to leave the room.

'Have you spoken to anyone in the last couple of days?' Dave demanded when she rejoined him in the office.

'I went shopping yesterday morning—' she began.

'No,' he interrupted. 'From here, I mean. Have you heard about the new appointment? A three-month exchange with Tony Phillips. Lucky beggar's ended up in a big city hospital in America. Seattle, I think.'

'Someone new here? In Accident and Emergency?'

'Yes,' Dave confirmed gleefully, his hazel eyes full of his customary humour. 'The Professor brought him round himself, yesterday afternoon.' He'd used the nickname of one of the consultants. 'Had all the staff in a flap.'

'You're not kidding,' a second voice chimed in, and a slim arm looped over Emma's shoulder as Diane West joined them. She licked her lips lasciviously. 'You wait till you see him. He's absolutely drop-dead gorgeous. All mean, moody and magnificent.' She giggled as Dave went pale and then red, his expression pained, almost as if he was trying to stop her from talking.

'What's the matter, Dave?' Emma teased. 'You're not jealous that you've finally got some competition in the department, are you? Perhaps you're afraid we'll all fall madly in love with him on sight—?'

'I certainly hope not,' a deep, accented voice said somewhere in the region of her left ear, and Emma spun on her heel to meet a pair of cold black eyes framed by the stark planes and hollows of the most sculpturally perfect face that she had ever seen on a man.

He's so tall, she thought, and blinked dazedly, her brain short-circuiting as she looked up at him.

He stood framed in the office doorway, so she could tell that he was at least eight inches taller than her own five and a half feet, with a whipcord leanness belied by the breadth of his shoulders. But it was his face that drew her eyes back—the golden olive tone of his skin, framed by jet-black hair lying flat against the contours of his skull and highlighted by the stark perfection of his fresh white coat.

'Nurse—' his dark eyes pierced her '—are you just here for a social visit or have you actually come to work? There is a room full of patients out there, waiting for attention.' He took one step back into the corridor and disappeared from view as silently as he'd appeared.

'Wow,' Diane mouthed, and mimed a swoon.

'Our new colleague?' With feigned calm, Emma glanced down at the fob-watch pinned to the front of her neat blue uniform and confirmed that she was still nearly fifteen minutes early for her shift. She was grateful for the years of practice which had helped her to hide her fierce response to him. He'd been there for less than a minute, but his presence had been so forceful that it almost seemed to linger in the room after he'd left.

'Yup!' Diane confirmed in an imitation American accent. 'That's our Dr Wolf.'

'Oh, please, Di, it might suit him down to the ground but that's too corny for words! You'll have to think of another nickname.' Emma tucked a couple of pens into her top pocket with hands still shaking from the sudden surge of adrenalin, and turned to follow his uncannily silent footsteps out towards the reception area.

'Honestly, Em, that's his real name.' Diane's tone stopped her in her tracks. 'His name really is Adam Wolf.'

Emma paused long enough to laugh with delight. 'I'd heard that certain pressure groups in America were pushing for compulsory product labelling and warning notices on dangerous substances, but I hadn't realised they'd taken the idea quite so far!'

She was still chuckling at intervals as, with her usual good-natured calm, she coped with the usual early-morning rush of patients from the nearby town and its surrounding housing estates.

By half past nine she had already organised to send a child with a large, discoloured, egg-shaped lump on his head up for a precautionary X-ray, after his mother had described his spectacular discovery that he could climb out of his high chair. She'd also dealt with three assorted ankle injuries and a fractured toe, and irrigated an eye full of sawdust for an over-enthusiastic amateur carpenter.

Her next patient was a very shaky elderly woman who'd fallen while shopping, and she was just wheeling her towards a vacant cubicle to attend to her various scrapes and bruises when there was a cry for help behind her.

'Nurse! Somebody...!' The young woman who'd been sitting patiently with a fidgety baby on her lap was clutching the child frantically in her arms and racing towards the reception desk. 'My baby can't breathe!'

Emma was the first one to reach her and plucked the struggling, red-faced youngster out of her arms and whirled into the emergency room, flinging questions over her shoulder as she went.

'Why did you bring him to the hospital? Was he having difficulty breathing?' To Emma's concern the child's face was taking on a blue tinge, the cyanosis showing her how severely his airway must be obstructed.

'No! It wasn't him... He was OK.' The poor mother's replies were almost incoherent. 'I only came here to bring my friend in because she had a fall... Oh, help him! Please do something...'

Her frantic words faded into the background as Emma concentrated fiercely on the child in her arms, her fingers flying to check his mouth for a small toy or any other obvious obstruction.

She was desperately conscious of his racing pulse and the terror in his eyes as she forced herself to focus, even managing to block out her awareness of the tall man who had just entered the room.

Suddenly she *knew* what was the matter and swiftly turned the child over so that he straddled her arm, with his head lower than his trunk. Quickly sitting down on the nearest chair, she supported his jaw and chest with her hand and rested the weight of her forearm along her thigh.

Four times she brought the heel of her other hand

down smartly between his shoulderblades, then she rolled him face up on her lap to deliver four chest thrusts.

Before she could open his mouth to look for a small foreign body in his throat, he coughed violently and a small white button landed several feet away on the floor, to the accompaniment of an indignant wail.

'Good enough,' a deep voice murmured in a transatlantic accent, and Emma's concentration was broken. She'd known that he was there ready to help, but she'd also known, somehow, that he would allow her to do what was necessary without interference.

'Thank you. Oh, thank you.' The child's mother swooped to wrap the sobbing youngster in her arms, tears pouring down her own white face as she cuddled him against her shoulder.

'He should be fine now.' Emma stroked his silky curls and patted his little shoulder. 'If you take him through to the reception area I'll send one of the nurses to fetch you a drink while you catch your breath.'

She directed her out of the door and turned to retrieve the offending button, only to find it displayed on one lean male palm.

'How did you know what was wrong?' His voice was gentle but his dark eyes were piercing, probing.

'I…' Emma found her gaze hopelessly snared and her thoughts stumbled frantically. 'I saw the damp place on the mother's blouse where the baby had been chewing…the place where the button was missing…'

She tore her eyes away, suddenly afraid that some-how he *knew* that she wasn't telling the truth. It was totally impossible, but those eyes seemed so mesmer-ising…as if he could see into her head, as if he could read her thoughts.

'Emma?' a voice called from the corridor.

'Coming,' she replied with a silent sigh of relief, and threw him a brief smile as she pushed her way through the doors to speak to one of the junior nurses. She gave a quick shudder as the door closed behind her, grateful to escape his presence. He was far too…too knowing…

'We've got a mum out here with a toddler who might have taken her grandmother's diuretic pills,' the young woman reported as she matched her swift pace to Emma's. 'She found her little girl surrounded by them but doesn't know how many she might have eaten.'

'Has she brought the bottle with her?' Emma thrust the enveloping feeling of uneasiness behind her as she concentrated on the next problem.

'Yes.'

'Well, phone through to the poison unit in London and they'll tell you what the best course of action is. Then come and let me know what they say.'

She knew that he had come to stand behind her, although he hadn't touched her, hadn't even made a sound. It was almost as though she was sensitive to him in some way, as if he was surrounded by some sort of energy field…

'We have similar poison-control centres in the States—about a hundred and twenty of them.' His deep voice sent a shiver down her spine and she turned slowly to face him.

'What part of America do you come from?' Emma found herself asking, not certain what had prompted the question. All she knew was that she couldn't bear to stand near him in silence.

Silence was dangerous.

When she allowed silence to fall it was harder to keep control...

'The north-west,' he supplied, his dark eyes unwavering on her face.

'S-Seattle, wasn't it?' she stammered, desperate to keep the conversation going until she could find some way to escape.

He nodded. 'That's where I was working. Look, is there anywhere I can get a cup of *real* coffee?'

'Unlikely.' Emma chuckled briefly at the disgusted expression which crossed his face, and glanced down at the time. 'Look, I'm due for a coffee-break any minute now. I could make you a fresh cup of decent instant...'

She stopped speaking and bit her tongue, horrified to hear what she'd said. Where had the words come from? She didn't want to spend any more time with this man than she had to. He frightened her in ways she didn't understand.

'Contradiction in terms,' he said, with a scowl, breaking into her scurrying thoughts. 'There's no such thing as *decent* instant coffee but if it's the only alternative to the grey dishwater I tried in the canteen this morning, lead on.'

As if he knew that she was looking for an excuse to get away from him and was deliberately foiling it, he turned to gesture politely for her to precede him along the corridor.

It was as he turned his head and the lights above struck blue gleams from his intensely black hair that, for the first time, Emma realised the thick, straight strands weren't just slicked back but were long enough to be tied at the base of his skull with a narrow leather thong.

She was sure that she hadn't made a sound at the startling discovery, but he turned his head sharply towards her as though she'd spoken, one eyebrow raised in a challenging arch.

'Something wrong?'

'Er, no.' Emma dragged her eyes away hurriedly and concentrated on reaching the staffroom. She could still feel the residue of heat in her cheeks as she pushed the door open and made her way to the kitchenette in the corner.

'How do you like it?' she threw over her shoulder, all too conscious of his silent presence in the room behind her.

'Strong and black, please.'

'Sugar? Or are you sweet enough without—?' She could have bitten her tongue off when she heard herself voice the teasing phrase, and the heat of embarrassment raced into her cheeks. What on earth was she thinking of, to say such a thing to—?

His sudden laughter drew her head round sharply and she was startled by the appreciative gleam in his dark eyes, his teeth very white and even against the coppery tone of his skin.

'Sweet enough without.' He threw the words back at her, his smile lingering to soften the planes and angles of his face for the first time.

'Sorry it's only instant.' Emma held out the hand-thrown pottery mug. 'At least it's one of the better brands, and it always seems to taste less like cardboard out of these mugs.' She turned to add a splash of milk to her own mug then leant back against the counter to take the first sip.

'Take the weight off your feet while you've got the chance,' he murmured as he lowered himself into an elderly leather-look armchair and stretched his long legs out in front of him to cross them at the ankles. He slid down in the seat until his head rested against the back, his elbows planted on each arm of the chair as he cradled the bottom of the mug on the buckle of his plaited leather belt.

Emma perched on the arm of the matching chair, unable to relax. There was something about this big, silent man that kept her on edge—something almost predatory that made her as wary as if she were the potential prey of the powerful creature whose name he bore.

She tried to fix her gaze on the speckled blue-grey

glaze of her coffee mug but was unable to help the
way her eyes kept straying towards him.

Each time she dragged them back to concentrate
anew on the swirls and dips on the curving pottery,
but each time she lost the battle, and she found herself
measuring the length and power of the legs stretching
out towards her, their long muscles barely camou-
flaged by neatly pressed black trousers. Under the
cover of a loose-weave white linen shirt, his taut waist
widened out into a deep chest and broad shoulders, all
framed by the white coat splayed open on each side
of him.

When her disobedient gaze finally reached the
corded length of his deeply tanned neck and the ele-
gant symmetry of his face, she found his dark eyes
waiting for her.

'You disapprove?'

The words were spoken softly but she had no difficulty hearing them or understanding the challenge
they contained—it was almost as if they were reaching
her brain without her needing to hear them first.

'Disapprove?' she repeated, her voice just a little
unsteady in spite of her efforts.

What was happening to her? Was it the after-effects
of the nightmare making her feel so off balance in his
presence, or was it a result of the concentration she'd
had to use to help the little boy choking on the button?

'Of long hair on men,' he pursued calmly.

'No!' she denied instantly as she relived her initial
appreciation of how his hair suited him, then she col-

oured as she realised what her vehemence could imply. 'I mean…in this hospital we have various members of staff, including a Sikh and a couple of Rastafarians, with different ethnic origins and hairstyles…' She knew that she was babbling but somehow couldn't halt the avalanche of words.

'Once upon a time it would probably have caused a problem with the hospital authorities but the various equal-rights groups…' Her earnest voice died away as she caught the glimpse of humour in his dark eyes, a stray gleam of gold where she had expected only blackness.

'So,' he drawled softly, 'we both obey the rules and keep our hair tied out of the way at work.' One corner of his mouth lifted in a wry smile.

Emma found herself gazing at him as she tried to imagine what he would look like when he let his hair loose. Was it fine and silky or thick and coarse? It was unlikely that it would spring into riotous waves as her own did when she took out the pins, but would probably hang either side of the lean planes of his face in straight dark sheets like…

'Oh!' She gave a slight gasp as recognition swept over her.

'Yes.' He nodded, his eyes darkly watchful. 'I'm what used to be called a Red Indian. Now they call us native Americans or American Indians.'

'What do *you* call yourself?' Emma challenged quietly, sensing his ambivalence over the direction of the conversation.

'Blackfoot,' he said, his voice filled with innate pride.

'Do you—?'

Before she could complete the question the door swung open and one of the younger nurses stuck her head round.

'Emma? Sorry to disturb you but you said you wanted me to report back when I'd spoken to the poisons unit.'

'Ah, yes.' Emma forced herself to concentrate. 'What did they advise?'

'They said to tell the mother to keep an eye on her little girl, but unless she started passing water a lot or feeling drowsy she would probably be fine.'

'Have you told her?'

'Yes.' She smiled and her eyes flicked briefly towards the silent occupant of the other chair. 'She was very relieved. Said she didn't know whether to hug her little girl or tell her off for worrying her so much.'

The door swung shut behind her as she returned to her duties.

'You believe in starting as you mean to go on?' His deep voice drew her eyes back to him as she was trying to think of a graceful way to leave the room without appearing to run away.

'In what way?' She swirled the last, rapidly cooling mouthfuls of coffee in the bottom of the cup, keeping her eyes on the patterns it made so that she wasn't tempted to look for the fleeting expressions crossing his face.

'The new breed of nurses,' he clarified. 'Highly trained professionals in their own right, able to take charge of many situations without needing direction from doctors.'

'In some fields the nurses are now more highly qualified than the doctors they're officially working under,' Emma agreed. 'Are you finding the situation very different here from what you left in—?'

'Emma?' Another head appeared around the edge of the door. 'Nurse Noone said to tell you Helen has been sent home with a migraine.'

'OK,' Emma smiled at the messenger and sent her on her way as she stood up. 'Damn,' she muttered under her breath. 'Now we'll really be pushed tonight.'

'Problem?' Adam Wolf straightened up to his full height and relinquished his mug into her outstretched hand.

'Only the age-old problem of too much work and staff off sick...' Emma rinsed the mugs out and upended them on the draining-rack before she turned to leave the temporary haven of the staffroom.

A long arm reached over her shoulder to push the door open and held it for her to walk through.

Emma flicked a shy smile up at him, unconsciously turning slightly as she passed him, to make sure that she didn't brush against him.

Over the years the manoeuvre had become such an ingrained habit of hers that she hardly realised she was doing it. As a child she had found it was the only way she could prevent herself from being mentally swamped by the feelings she picked up from other people when they touched her.

Suddenly she was swept by an overwhelming feeling of cold anger, and she became conscious that the powerful body beside her had grown rigid with disapproval. Even the air around them seemed to have grown chilly.

'You're quite safe, you know. It's not catching,' he snapped curtly as he glared down from his superior height, his tone caustic.

'What isn't?' Emma lifted stunned eyes towards him in total bewilderment. She shook her head, her thoughts suddenly a chaotic jumble, as if her brain was filled with static.

'The colour of my skin.' His eyes pierced her like twin lasers, his expression cold and hard as he turned away from her to stride down the corridor.

'Wait,' Emma called, but either he didn't hear her or he ignored the plea in her voice. 'Dammit,' she cursed under her breath, and pressed her lips together as she glanced towards the rapidly filling reception area.

She didn't have time to try to catch him now, but as soon as she got the chance she would tell him that her reaction hadn't been one of aversion—at least, not aversion to him as a person. She would have to find the words to explain that she avoided contact with everyone, regardless of the colour of their skin. Surely

she could find some way of telling him without having
to reveal the reason why...

Over the next few hours Emma made several attempts
to speak to Adam Wolf, but every time she went to
approach him he managed to disappear. It was some
while before she realised that his evasiveness was deliberate—that he was avoiding being anywhere near
her.

As she gathered her belongings up, ready to go
home at the end of her shift, she felt tired and dispir-
ited.

The day's work had been no worse than that of any
other summer Friday in a hospital situated close to a
major motorway, but she was weighed down by a deep
sadness that her unconscious body language had killed
the first tender shoots of the fragile friendship which
had been springing up between herself and the solemn
Adam Wolf.

She had a feeling that he was as solitary as she was,
and she could hardly lie to herself about the strength
of the attraction she'd felt for him in spite of her usual
wariness.

Now he believed that Emma had been repulsed by
his revelation of his Blackfoot heritage, when nothing
could have been further from the truth. She had been
attracted to him as a man from the first moment she
had turned and seen him standing in the office doorway—more attracted than she'd allowed herself to be

in several years, perhaps in her whole life, and it wasn't just a physical attraction.

For the first time she had met a man who called to her on more than one level, someone who had challenged the cold stillness she'd cultivated inside herself ever since she had parted company with Richard two years ago.

For the rest of the evening she fought a silent battle with herself, vacillating between leaving the situation with the all too fascinating Dr Wolf just as it was and making an effort to try to set the record straight.

'He's only here on a three-month exchange,' she muttered as she ploughed through the hated pile of ironing. 'There's no point in letting myself get involved with him. He'll be on his way back to Seattle by the time we get to know each other...' She pulled a face as her heart sank. 'That's if he ever lets me get close enough to explain why I didn't want him to touch me.'

She drew in a deep, unhappy breath as she replayed the searing memories of the last time she'd tried to explain the unexplainable.

'That's always supposing that it's worth making the effort,' she grumbled later as she finally slid her feet under the covers and settled herself into bed. 'If I get the chance to tell him why, there's no guarantee that he'll believe me, and if he does and reacts the same way as Richard did...'

Misery settled over her as she imagined the intrigued disbelief if the rest of her colleagues were to find out what had been going on under their noses ever since she'd joined the staff at St Lawrence's. It had grown so bad last time that she'd moved out of the area completely, lucky to land her present job so quickly.

Was it worth taking the chance that she might have to move on again...?

Her tangled thoughts didn't allow her to sleep well, so that she was already awake the next morning when she was overwhelmed by a terrible feeling of hopelessness.

For the second time in as many days her control was shattered by a stranger's torment.

At first she fought to block the avalanche of emotion but the effort was useless, leaving her weak and trembling, her arms wrapped around herself as if she were trying to stop herself from flying apart into a million jagged pieces.

Finally she bowed to the inevitable and stopped fighting, allowing her body to relax bonelessly as she closed her eyes and concentrated on her sensations. Perhaps, now, two years on, she would be able to cope with them better; perhaps this time she could find some way to control what was happening...

CHAPTER TWO

SOMEWHERE, someone was fighting demons. Somewhere, far too close for comfort, there was someone being torn apart by the pull of two opposing forces.

Emma felt her own body being taken over by the spillover of emotions, her pulse rate and breathing accelerating as they reacted to the enormous tension.

Desolation.

Emma was overwhelmed by the terrible feelings of loneliness and isolation that she was picking up from this unknown person. Someone had a choice to make, and it was tearing them apart.

She concentrated fiercely. It didn't matter how hard she tried, she had no mental image of the person whose thoughts were invading her life, and no clear understanding of the nature of the awful dilemma he or she was facing.

It was so frustrating.

In the past she had been able to decipher enough about the people with whom she made a mental connection to at least have the satisfaction of knowing when their problems had been resolved. This time both the person and the nature of his or her dichotomy were a complete mystery to her.

Suddenly, as if someone had thrown an electrical switch, the connection was broken and Emma was left feeling as if she'd been hit by a bus.

She lay still for several moments as her breathing steadied and her heartbeat slowed, then she released a long sigh of relief.

'Gone,' she breathed in disbelief as she searched the corners of her mind. 'Completely gone.' And she finally allowed herself to relax.

'Well,' she murmured as she rolled over to the edge of the bed and sat up, 'whoever you were and whatever your problem was, I hope that's the last I hear of you.' And she padded through to the bathroom for a reviving shower.

Emma had been on duty for a couple of hours when the emergency call came through.

'RTA. Four. One critical,' she called over her shoulder, knowing that the rest of the team would swing into action with practised efficiency.

She could hear the various sounds which told her that the trauma rooms were being readied while she held the phone link to the paramedic in the ambulance with one hand and jotted notes as fast as she could with the other.

'MVA?' a deep voice queried as she put the receiver down, the dark honey of its accent pouring over her.

There was no way she could delay the inevitable, much as she wished that they could have had some privacy for this meeting, but privacy was a luxury not readily available in such a busy department.

'A what?' She barely remembered what she was asking as she turned to look up at his midnight-dark eyes for the first time in twenty-four hours, and found his gaze chillingly expressionless.

'MVA—motor vehicle accident,' he elaborated.

'RTA—road traffic accident,' she parroted, a sick emptiness opening up inside her. 'Different terminology, same emergency.' And they turned simultaneously as they heard the sirens arriving.

'Are radiology on stand-by?' He was all efficiency.

Emma nodded. 'And the lab's ready for typing and cross-matching blood,' she confirmed just as briskly as they made their way towards the first patient, who was being wheeled through the doors.

'Male. Twenty-nine years old,' the paramedic began reciting as soon as they arrived. 'Blood pressure one-ten over seventy, pulse one-oh-eight, respiration twenty-four. Head-on collision caused impact with steering wheel. Chest pain.' He relinquished the upraised bag of intravenous saline to the nurse who took his place beside the patient.

Within seconds Emma was supervising the removal of the man's clothing to allow a closer examination.

'Mr Taylor?' She spoke above the escalating noise in the department. 'Do you hurt anywhere else than in your chest?'

'Knee,' he gasped through the clear mask covering his nose and mouth. 'Hit my knee…'

'OK.' She covered his hand with her own gloved one in a spontaneous gesture of sympathy. 'We'll take a look at it as soon as we've got your clothes out of the way. Is there anything else?'

He tried to shake his head, obviously forgetting that he was in a collar and strapped to a backboard, and groaned. 'Everything hurts,' he said in a muffled voice, 'but nothing else in particular.'

'Ribs,' Adam Wolf confirmed as his long fingers probed carefully over the man's chest and abdomen. 'No suspicious sounds from his lungs, no apparent internal damage. Patella's a mess, but it doesn't look as if any of the long bones are involved…'

In minutes the team had prepared Mr Taylor for the X-rays required to rule out spinal injury and for the set to be taken of his chest and knee.

The operating theatre staff was warned that he was on his way just as the sound of the second ambulance filled the air.

As the doors opened Emma had her first glimpse of the paramedic fighting with the occupant of the trolley.

'Mel? Where's Mel?' A blood-soaked arm flailed about as the young man tried to push himself upright. 'What have you done with Mel?'

'Mr Price.' The paramedic narrowly avoided having his clipboard sent flying as he tried to calm his patient. 'John, calm down. She's coming in a minute, I promise.'

The handover between the ambulance men and the A and E staff was chaotic, with voices growing louder and louder as they all tried to pass on essential information over the patient's progressively violent language.

'Mr Price.' Emma ducked under the IV line leading into the back of his hand and positioned herself out of range at his head. 'Please, Mr Price, listen to me.' She laid one hand across his forehead and managed to catch his free hand in the other.

He was a big man with very well-developed muscles, and she doubted that she would have been able to hold him if she hadn't caught his injured arm. As it was, she tightened her grip and concentrated, dismissing everything from her mind except the need to calm him down.

'Listen, John.' She leant forward cautiously, keeping a firm grasp on his wrist and allowing her voice to drop almost to a whisper, as if she were going to tell him an important secret.

'Listen,' she repeated softly, the word a soft susurration in the bustle of the room.

As if by magic, everyone else in the room lowered their voices too, no one wanting to miss out on what she was going to say.

'Can you hear it, Mr Price?' Emma whispered right beside his ear, her eyes suddenly catching Adam

Wolf's dark gaze concentrating on her as she bent over awkwardly at the top of the trolley.

'Hear what?' The hoarse voice of the patient broke into her preoccupation with the grudging gleam of approval that she had seen in Adam's eyes at the other end of the trolley.

'The ambulance siren,' Emma murmured confidingly. 'It's just arriving with Mel. Listen.'

While the patient was preoccupied with listening to the siren Emma gave a nod to the rest of the team. With Mr Price finally calmed down, they could get to work on preparing him for the stitching up of the deep gash running down his arm from elbow to wrist.

'Nurse?' Worried blue eyes looked up at her as she kept her calming hand on his head, his macho bluster vanquished by the genuine concern on his boyish face. 'Will you find out what they're doing to Mel? It's her legs... She was trapped and...and I think she's hurt them pretty bad...'

As Emma watched, a single tear trickled into the dusty blond hair at his temple, and she shifted her hand on his forehead just enough to smooth the betraying dampness away.

'Only if you promise to behave yourself,' she bargained teasingly, giving his shoulder a squeeze. 'If you don't do what this lot tell you, I'll go off for a coffee-break instead.' She glanced up from her position at his head and received a brief nod from Adam as he completed his examination.

'Nurse Sullivan—' He addressed her formally in a normal tone of voice and Emma knew from her brief glimpse of his expression that it was for their patient's benefit '—when you see Mel, you can tell her that Mr Price will have collected an interesting scar but that everything else appears to be in working order.'

'Certainly, Doctor. At once.' She smiled down at her patient and, ducking out from behind the drip stand, walked swiftly towards the trolley just entering the trauma unit.

The young woman was strapped to a backboard and the white gleam of the collar surrounding her neck seemed to leach every vestige of colour from her face; her eyes were tightly closed above the clear plastic of the mask over her nose and mouth.

'Mel Price. Twenty-four-year-old female. Shunt injury. Both knees, possibly both hips involved. Blood pressure ninety over seventy, pulse one-eleven, respiration eighteen.'

'Hello, Mel.' Emma took the slender wrist between her fingers and monitored the pulse as soon as the backboard she was strapped to had been transferred off the ambulance trolley.

'Where's John?' Deep blue eyes flicked open to fix insistently on Emma's. 'Is…is he all r-right? Have you s-seen him?'

'Calm down.' Emma soothed the fingers clutching frantically at her arm. 'He's here and he's safe.' She chuckled. 'In fact the doctor told me to give you a message when you got here.'

'A m-message?' The young woman caught her breath and winced as she was positioned ready for X-ray.

'Yes. He said to tell you that apart from a rather interesting scar on his arm—which, knowing men, he'll probably boast about for the rest of his life— everything else is in perfect working order.'

Emma watched the frightened young woman relax as the message sank in, and gave her hand a reassuring squeeze before she returned to business.

'Mel? We need to get a picture of you to make sure you haven't damaged your hips. Can you tell me the date of your last period?'

'Why…why do you need to know that?'

'It's a precaution we have to take, just in case you're pregnant. X-raying your knees isn't a problem but we need to take a picture of this area.' Emma gently touched the badly bruised area at the side of one hip and slid her hand across to the other side. 'And if you're in the early stages of pregnancy it can harm the baby.'

'I don't…I'm not…'

'Nurse.' Adam Wolf's voice rumbled in her ear. 'Her husband says she's not pregnant. She's on the Pill.'

His voice sent a strange shiver up her back, to raise

the soft hairs on the nape of her neck, but that wasn't the reason why she suddenly stiffened.

When he'd spoken, her hand had still been resting on Mel's slender abdomen, and now her eyes flew to meet the obsidian darkness of the tall man standing just behind her shoulder.

'Is he sure?' she murmured distractedly as she tried to concentrate on what her sixth sense was telling her. 'She hasn't had a stomach bug or...or taken any antibiotics recently, has she?'

'What are you thinking?' His eyes had sharpened on her, their gaze so intense that she almost felt as if he was trying to see into her head.

'Just...just double-checking.' She dragged her eyes away and bent towards the pale figure of their patient. 'Mel? Are you sure there isn't any chance that you might be pregnant?'

'I...I don't know. I...I might be...' The words were a breathy whisper as her cheeks gained a slight tinge of pink. 'I had an abscess under a tooth and the dentist gave me some tablets...'

'Antibiotics?' Adam demanded gently.

'I think so...' Her forehead pleated as she tried to concentrate.

'Right.' He straightened up decisively. 'We'll warn X-ray to use a shield, just in case you are pregnant, and then we'll take it from there.'

Emma studiously avoided his gaze as she took care of her frightened patient, but she couldn't help being aware that he was watching her, the impact of his dark eyes almost as potent as a physical touch.

She didn't need extra-sensory perception to know that he was wondering about her.

'Dammit!' she muttered under her breath as she saw the last victim from the crash leave the department for further treatment elsewhere in the hospital. Why did there have to be two incidents so close together and both of them when he was near enough to watch what she was doing?

It wasn't the first time she'd railed against the circumstances—accident of birth, fate, whatever it was—that had doomed her to go through life sensitive to people in a way few others were.

Most of the time she could almost forget about it— at least, she had been able to for the last two years. It was just her bad luck that she seemed to have lost her control over it just when they'd acquired a very keen-eyed doctor in the department.

If she wasn't going to find herself in a very uncomfortable position, she would just have to keep her fingers crossed for the next few days that nothing else happened to draw Adam Wolf's attention to her. The alternative didn't bear thinking about.

In the meantime, she decided, with a determined tilt to her chin as she followed him towards the staffroom for a much needed cup of coffee, she had some unfinished business to settle with Dr Adam Wolf!

'Is there any water left in the kettle?' She directed

her question at his broad back as she crossed the freshly polished composite floor, her soft-soled shoes almost soundless as she negotiated the informal groups of chairs on her way towards him at the kitchenette in the corner.

The delicious aroma of coffee struck her before she was halfway there and she drew it in with a deep breath of appreciation.

'I don't know about water in the kettle, but there's an extra cup here if you'd like it.' He turned around to show her the carafe of dark liquid in his hand.

'Where did that come from? Did someone in the hospital hierarchy have a brainstorm and take pity on us?'

'No such luck.' His dark eyes glanced briefly in her direction. 'I brought this in myself as I seem to be spending more time here than at home.'

'So that's *real* coffee, is it?' she challenged, deliberately reminding him of their previous conversation on the subject.

'The real McCoy.' He poured a steady stream of the rich dark brew into one of the pottery mugs, raising one eyebrow at her as he held up the bottle of milk.

Emma nodded and watched as he added a thin stream and stirred it around for a second.

'Here.' He held the mug out towards her in one tanned hand. 'I'll forgive you the sacrilege of putting milk in it on the grounds that you don't know any better.'

To Emma's relief, the harsh expression he'd worn in her presence had softened slightly and she reached out to take the mug from him.

Without thinking about it, she curved her fingers around the top rim of the mug to lift it out of his grasp without coming into contact with his fingers.

'For God's sake…!'

His violent exclamation made her jerk her hand and nearly spill the scalding liquid. Only her quick reaction allowed her to step aside to allow the stream of coffee to splatter harmlessly on the floor.

'Did you burn yourself?' In one lithe movement he was crouching in front of her, lifting the hem of her uniform to check her legs.

'No. It missed me—no thanks to you!' Emma subdued a shudder which was caused as much by the proximity of the powerful man bending down in front of her as it was by shock at her near escape. 'Why on earth did you shout like that? No wonder I jumped.' Her voice was shaky but the words were full of self-righteous accusation as she stepped back from him.

'I didn't shout *at* you.' He straightened up to glare down at her from his full height.

'You did—'

'It was your reaction,' he continued, totally ignoring her attempt to contradict him. 'That's the second time you've made a song and dance about going anywhere near me. Have you any idea how insulting it is?'

Emma gasped and her cheeks reddened as she found

her horrified gaze trapped by the Stygian darkness
of his.

'It wasn't…I wasn't…' she stumbled. 'Oh, Lord…'
She glanced helplessly from his eyes down to the drip-
ping mug in her quivering hand and back up again.
She had wanted a chance to explain what had happened last time, had deliberately followed him in here
to engineer a conversation, and it seemed as if all
she'd done was make matters worse.

'Give me that.' He reached out for the mug. 'You'd
better sit down before you fall down.' One hand
wrapped delicately around the curve of the pottery so
that his lean fingers covered her own slender ones,
taking her completely by surprise.

It was the shock, she told herself as a bolt of light-
ning shot through her at the contact. She wasn't in
control of herself and *that* was why she couldn''t
block him out.

Years of practice helped her to keep her expression
bland as she was flooded by the overwhelming reality
of touching Adam Wolf for the first time, that same
control allowing her to release her hold on the mug
and begin to draw her hand away.

What she really wanted to do was snatch it out of
his grasp and cradle it against her with her other hand,
as if it had been burnt by the contact.

All the control in the world couldn't prevent her soft
sigh of relief as he took the mug away and set it down
on the coffee-table. Gratefully, she sank into one cor-

ner of the couch and tucked her shaky legs out of the way.

'Why?'

The single word emerged in the room almost as an accusation, his fierce gaze never leaving her as he sat himself in the chair facing her seat.

Emma sat mute, her brain seething with a chaotic mixture of thoughts and feelings, none of them coherent enough to voice.

'*Is* it my colour?' The words were spoken as calmly as if her answer were unimportant, but Emma knew it wasn't; in spite of determined efforts to block him out, his tension was reaching her in waves, each one stronger than the last.

'No.' She looked straight at him, fixing her silvery grey eyes firmly on the darkness of his as she filled the word with conviction.

His scepticism reached her then and she hurried into speech in an attempt to convince him, knowing without his having to say a word that this was an old wound.

'Honestly.' She held her hands out in a placatory gesture, leaning towards him as if to lend weight to her words. 'It's nothing to do with your colour or...or the fact you have long hair—'

'Then what is it?' he demanded, his low voice rough to her ears. 'Why do you shy away from contact with me as if I'll contaminate you in some way? What is it about me that offends your delicate sensibilities?'

'Nothing,' Emma declared earnestly. 'It's not you…' She shook her head while she tried to find the words to explain without revealing the full extent of her problem.

'Is it men in general?' he suggested. 'Were you attacked and it's left you frightened of the rest of us? Or—' a sudden thought struck him and he blinked '—or do you prefer women to men?'

'No,' she shook her head in violent repudiation. 'It's nothing like that.' Her teeth worried at her lower lip as she realised that, far from being straightened out, the situation was growing more complicated by the minute.

'It's everybody.' The words finally escaped her precarious control. 'It's not just you…I can't touch anybody…'

The ensuing silence was profound as his face registered his shock at her outburst.

'But…that's ridiculous!' The dark slashes of his eyebrows were drawn into a fierce frown as he focused his mind on her incomprehensible words. 'You're a nurse, for God's sake; you're touching people all day long.'

'That's different,' Emma said flatly.

'How?' he demanded. 'How is it different?'

'I… I don't know. It just is.'

'Have you been for any help? Perhaps a psychiatrist might be able to…'

Emma felt the familiar wave of revulsion sweep

over her as she remembered the first time she'd been *persuaded* to see a psychiatrist, willing to try anything for the man she'd loved.

Perhaps it had been sheer bad luck that the one she'd seen had treated her like some sort of freak... 'All in the name of scientific research, of course,' he'd said. 'It will make such an interesting paper when it's published in the *Lancet*.'

Whatever the rights and wrongs of it—and she had found out during her nursing training that it had been very wrong—she had sworn that it would never happen again.

'Yes—' her voice was hard '—I've seen a psychiatrist, and no, it didn't help.'

'I'm sorry,' he said gently, his expression thoughtful when she caught his eyes on her white knuckles.

'Don't be,' she dismissed, with a shaky attempt at airiness, deliberately unclenching her fingers and leaving them to lie in her lap in a pretence of relaxation. 'I've worked out my own survival strategy and most of the time it works—'

'Doctor?'

Diane West's head appeared around the edge of the door to inform him that he was needed, and Emma could have hugged her.

She knew that it would be only a matter of time before Adam Wolf's agile brain started analysing the answers she'd given and realised how evasive she'd been. All she could hope was that his concentration on his work would push the details of their conversation out of his head so that he couldn't remember exactly what she'd said...

'Emma?'

As if she'd conjured him up, he stepped back into the room again, his dark eyes finding hers with worrying ease.

For a moment she was certain that he was going to take their conversation further, and her stomach tied itself into a tight knot.

'You did well today in all that bedlam.' A rare smile lit his eyes with golden gleams. 'It was a pleasure to work with you.' And he was gone.

'Well.' Emma flopped back into the corner of the couch, surprise at his sudden compliment robbing her of all strength—and it wasn't just the compliment.

'That smile ought to be registered as a deadly weapon,' she murmured while her pulse registered its after-effects, which were like the tremors following an earthquake. 'It's potent enough to cause serious heart damage.'

As she forced herself to her feet she chuckled at her own silliness, her heart immeasurably lighter after their talk in spite of the prospect that the topic would probably be resurrected when he'd had time to think about it.

At least she'd been able to convince him that his Blackfoot heritage wasn't the reason for her aversion to contact. In fact, if she was honest with herself, it made him all the more attractive.

In the meantime she had several more stressful hours to go before she could afford time to daydream about a dark-haired, dark-eyed man who could send her pulse rate off the end of the scale with a single smile.

Her return to the department coincided with the arrival of several patients looking decidedly green.

'We think we've got food poisoning,' the spokesman said as he ushered the sorry-looking group in.

'What do you think caused it?' Emma led them through the department as quickly as she could because one of their number was growing paler by the second.

'Fish,' he muttered as he grabbed the bowl that Emma held out towards him, and made immediate use of it.

'Did you *all* have fish?' She counted eleven heads as she handed each of them a bowl.

'Birthday party for Grandad,' one of the youngest victims volunteered. 'He doesn't like prawns, so he's OK. They were the biggest ones I've ever seen—'

'Shut up, Tim,' one of the others groaned just before he too was violently sick.

'Where did you have the party?' Emma directed the question to the group as a whole. 'I need to know where the prawns came from.'

'Eagle Hotel, just outside town. Near the golf

course,' someone supplied. 'We had to wait ages to be served and then this happens...'

Emma organised for extra chairs to be carried through and called Adam to check her findings.

'We need to notify the appropriate authorities so they can send an inspector round to the hotel kitchen before the contaminated food can be disposed of,' he detailed in an aside to Emma. 'I'll leave it to you to sort that one out—you know the proper departments to contact in England better than I do.'

'Fine.' Emma smiled. 'In the meantime, I'm a bit worried about a couple of the victims. I think they're beginning to get dehydrated, and while they're still being sick we can't give them anything by mouth.'

'Let's work our way round the room to check each of them in turn. Any that are beginning to look a bit distressed can have an IV unit of saline to help them through. Luckily, this sounds far more like an outbreak of staphylococcal food poisoning than salmonella, so it'll be of a much shorter duration. Either way, we'll send some samples up to the lab for identification— the confirmation of the diagnosis can then be used in any prosecution against the hotel.'

'Let's just keep our fingers crossed that the hotel doesn't have any other parties booked while this lot are in residence here,' Emma muttered under her breath. 'It could end up looking like a scene from a disaster movie.'

For the next couple of hours there was a constant

stream of patients between their makeshift ward and the nearby toilets as diarrhoea alternated with vomiting, and the nurses all took turns in ministering to the sorry party.

'Next time, I'll cook the food myself,' one of the women declared. 'I'd rather be worn out preparing a menu we'll all enjoy than exhausted by getting rid of food someone else has made.'

'And it cost more,' one of the men grumbled, prompting a weak round of laughter.

'Now I know you're getting better, if you've started griping about the cost rather than how bad you feel,' Emma teased.

'Seriously,' she continued as she removed the last of the IV lines, 'as soon as you feel able to cope at home, it would be a good idea if you can ring for the members of the party who escaped all this and get them to take you home. You'll feel better if you can lie down comfortably in your own home and, really, there isn't a lot more we can do for you here—you're all well on the mend.'

Within minutes one of them had ventured out with a list of telephone numbers, and the rest of them started gathering up their belongings.

'Thank you for looking after us so well,' one of the older gentlemen said. His face was still pale but his voice had lost its former tremor. 'You've all been very kind to us and we're grateful.' His smile held a touch of devilry as he continued, 'I hope you don't mind if we say that, in spite of your kindness, we'd rather not meet you again.'

'Uncle!' several voices remonstrated, but Emma smiled.

'As long as you don't mind us saying that we hope we never see you here again either!' And she shook their hands as they filed past her and out to the waiting cars.

Emma had no sooner returned the room to order than there was a warning that an ambulance was bringing in the victims of another poisoning.

'Suspected carbon monoxide. Two adults and two children,' Diane relayed. 'I'm due off duty in a few minutes but I'll stay on if you need me.'

'Thanks, Di.' Emma glanced down at the time. 'If you can hang on until we see how bad they are...?'

The whole team was lined up and waiting as the ambulance drew up at the entrance. Each trolley was ready for the transfer of a patient, with a cylinder of one hundred per cent oxygen waiting with a non-rebreathing mask.

'Oh, my God,' Emma breathed when she saw how young the two unconscious children were. 'They're just little scraps.' And she supervised their immediate transfer to the larger trauma room.

'Can you spare enough nurses to cover each of them?' Adam's voice reached her over the hum and rhythmic bleeping of the monitoring equipment.

'Until they regain consciousness, certainly—barring

a major influx of casualties,' she agreed, and detailed a nurse to each member of the family.

'Do we know how long they were exposed?' His murmur just behind her confirmed her feeling that he was nearby. It was almost as if her skin was sensitive to his presence, as if he was surrounded by some sort of force field that her body could detect.

'N-not really.' Emma scolded herself for her lack of concentration. This was hardly the time to be thinking about her reaction to Adam Wolf. 'The paramedic said it was probably the gas boiler they used for heating water. Apparently it was the only item in use.'

'Who raised the alarm? One of the parents?'

'No. A neighbour.' She chuckled. 'She came storming round to complain that their cat had come in through the wrong cat flap and had been sick all over their new carpet. When she couldn't get a reply in spite of knowing the family was home, she peered in through the window.'

'Sometimes it's quite frightening when you realise how important coincidence is in our lives.' His deep voice flowed softly in the muted bustle of the room. 'If the cat hadn't been affected, if it hadn't made it outside, if it hadn't gone in the wrong house, if it hadn't been sick, if the neighbour hadn't decided to go to complain...' He allowed the list to end with a shrug.

'When you look at those two—' Emma nodded towards the little bodies '—it doesn't bear thinking about.' She shuddered.

By the time she was ready to hand over to the next shift, all four members of the family were conscious and had been admitted for overnight observation.

Emma was glad. She would have hated to go home without knowing that they were all recovering well, especially the little ones.

She kicked off her shoes and flopped back on her bed. Her feet were throbbing with tiredness and her calves were tight and aching.

'Still, a good night's sleep and I'll be ready for another shift,' she announced to the ceiling as she tried to summon the energy to go to the bathroom.

Lazily, she unfastened her clothing and stripped it off without leaving the soft comfort of the bed. It was all going to go into the laundry basket anyway, so what did it matter that it was landing in a heap on the floor?

The warmth of the August sunshine still lingered in the room as she lay naked on the soft cotton cover of her duvet, and she glanced idly down at herself.

'Too skinny,' she muttered as she took in the angles and points of her ribs and hips. 'The legs aren't bad, though.' She raised one slender foot in the air and pointed her toes to admire the shape of her calf and thigh, then she winced as the muscles complained. She

let the foot drop back onto the cushioned softness with
a thud.

'Heaven only knows where I got these from.' She
cupped her hands around the abundance of her breasts.
'There's a very voluptuous woman somewhere out
there who got the pair of bee stings I should have had.'
She giggled at the mental image, knowing in her heart
of hearts that she was rather proud of the unexpectedly
beautiful bounty.

'Now all I've got to do is find a man to appreciate
them…' She gave a snort. 'Except that's not the problem, is it? There are plenty of men who would want
to get their hands on these if they were given half a
chance—they just don't want the person they're attached to…'

Loneliness.

Emma jerked her hands away from herself in shock,
her face flaming with embarrassed heat. The intrusion
of another person's emotions into her head made her
feel as if someone had just walked into her room and
found her naked on the bed.

CHAPTER THREE

'GET OUT!' Emma shrieked breathlessly as she scrambled to cover her bare body with the duvet, pulling it right up under her chin just as if there really were an intruder in the room. 'Get out of my head!' And she pressed her fingers hard against her forehead as if she could force the thoughts away.

Loneliness. Longing.

The sensations poured through her like an avalanche, completely demolishing her puny defences. Whoever it was that kept breaking through her control hadn't solved his or her problem the other day. If anything, it was growing worse.

'I can't help you,' Emma moaned through gritted teeth as the familiar frustration gripped her. 'I can only hear you; I can't talk back.'

She remembered her attempts to communicate as a child, before she'd realised that none of her friends heard the same things she did. It had been some time before her mother had realised that her daughter had been afflicted with the family curse, and she'd tried to warn her what would happen—what had always happened to the women in her family.

Of course, Emma hadn't believed her. She'd felt

bound to pass on the 'information' she received about lost children and injured neighbours, until the notoriety had forced them to move.

Eventually she had learned to be discreet. She'd become more careful over whom she told and what she told them, but still she'd refused to believe that it could prevent her from having a normal life.

Until she'd met Richard and fallen in love...

Emma drew in a deep, shuddering breath. His rejection still hurt; his repudiation of her as a freak and his revulsion at the idea that she might be able to read his mind had left scars on her soul that might never heal.

Since then she'd been very cautious. Oh, she was friendly enough with people at the hospital, even joined in the occasional get-together for an engagement or a birthday, but she allowed no one any closer than that. Her mother had been right—it wasn't worth the heartbreak.

Isolation.

Why did she think of Adam Wolf when that emotion assailed her? He seemed a very solitary, self-contained person, it was true, but that could be because he was a newcomer in the department and his time among them was limited.

Need.

That certainly didn't make her think of Adam. She couldn't imagine him ever admitting to needing anyone. He was so strong—physically and mentally.

Unlike the poor soul crying out for contact.

How could she refuse? She knew that she couldn't reply. Then again, a child she'd 'heard' in a quarry all those years ago had somehow known that someone was coming, known that someone was there.

Emma settled herself under the duvet and made herself comfortable. Hesitantly she willed herself to relax, not knowing quite what to expect.

'I'm listening,' she whispered into the growing shadows of the room. 'I won't fight you any more.'

She lay quietly, a feeling of calm drifting over her as she finally gave in to the inevitable. Whoever was 'speaking' to her must be desperate, having tried so often to make contact even in the face of her repeated rebuffs.

Alone.

Emma jerked with sudden awareness as, without her usual shield, the emotion hit her at full force. She drew in a deep breath and allowed it to trickle slowly away, taking with it all her tension. Later she might regret what she was doing, but, just for the moment, it felt right.

'Not alone any more,' she breathed softly, and waited to see what would happen.

Thank you.

She was bathed in an incredible mixture of warmth and light, which flowed around her, inside and out, until she was filled with it.

For the first time Emma felt the weight of her inherited burden lift.

* * *

'Morning,' Dave greeted her as she arrived in the department the next day.

'Gorgeous, isn't it?' Emma agreed with a broad smile. 'No one would dare have an accident on such a lovely day, would they?'

'Optimist!' The accusation followed her as she went to deposit her bag and she chuckled. It was amazing the difference a good night's sleep had made to her outlook.

Not that she had expected to sleep well.

After her sudden capitulation to whomever had been plaguing her, she had expected to lie awake for hours. The last thing she had expected to happen was that she would drift off to sleep as easily as a newborn baby and wake with a smile on her face.

She felt good, she realised as she made her way back towards Reception with a spring in her step—and it wasn't just due to the beautiful weather either.

'Emma, are you half day today or tomorrow?' Dave queried as she arrived.

'Supposed to be today. Why? Do they need me to stay on?'

'Not as far as I know,' he temporised. 'It's my own fault for leaving it so late, but I'm hoping to do a swap with someone for tomorrow.'

'Sorry. Can't help.' She turned away and walked straight into a living, breathing wall.

'Oops!'

'Sorry!'

Adam Wolf grinned down at her as they each took a rapid backward step, and Emma's pulse leapt. That smile was definitely a lethal weapon!

'Are we so quiet in the department that we're having to supply our own casualties?' he joked, and continued on his way.

'Wow!' breathed one of the junior nurses who had just started work in A and E that morning. 'He's yummy!'

'Careful, Jilly,' Emma laughed. 'You'll end up picking carpet fluff off your tongue if you don't put it away.'

'Emma!' Jilly's cheeks went pink. 'You can't tell me he doesn't get you going too. And that accent!'

Emma sent her about her duties without commenting because it was true. She *was* attracted to Adam Wolf—had been from the first time she'd seen him—but the more she got to know about him, the more she realised that there was a great deal more to the man than the fact that he was a good-looking doctor.

'Nurse?'

Emma looked up as she was hailed by the motherly woman at the reception desk, and altered her direction.

'Can I help?' She addressed the couple standing by the desk when the receptionist indicated them.

'It's Holly. She hasn't been well for a couple of days and we thought it was just a summer cold, but she's been ever so sick…'

'Bring her through here.' Emma directed them into the smaller trauma room and signalled for Adam to be sent in as soon as he was free.

While she was waiting for him to arrive she took a detailed history and helped Holly's mother to take her child's clothing off.

As she worked she kept up a soothing conversation with the parents, but her eyes kept straying to the doorway every time she heard a noise as she waited for Adam to come. She had a funny feeling about this one.

'Doctor, this is Holly. She's three years old,' Emma began the moment that Adam arrived, handing him a disposable mask and fresh pair of gloves as soon as he entered the room.

For a second he paused, one eyebrow raised as his eyes sought hers, then he gave a brief nod and donned the mask and gloves.

'Holly's had a slightly raised temperature and has seemed as if she was getting a cold for the last couple of days,' Emma reported. 'About an hour ago she vomited and went very drowsy so her parents brought her straight in.'

'Well done. You did the right thing,' he murmured in a reassuring tone as he started his examination. 'Has she been in contact with any infectious illnesses like measles?'

'Not so far as we know,' her mother replied. 'She started play-group about six months ago and she's had the usual sort of colds and tummy upsets, but nothing serious. Not until this morning. She said her head hurt.'

'Had you noticed this rash?' Adam flipped back the blanket covering the youngster and indicated the blotchy areas starting to show against her pale skin.

'No.' The poor woman glanced towards her husband for confirmation. 'We looked at her neck when she said it didn't want to bend but we didn't see a rash.'

'Have you any other children?'

'Not yet. Holly's our first.'

Adam glanced up at Emma across the width of the trolley and nodded. She could only see the part of his face not covered by the disposable mask, but the concern in his eyes was unmistakable.

'I'm afraid we need to do some tests on Holly,' he began as Emma watched carefully for the reaction of the little girl's parents.

'Do you know what's the matter with her?' the anxious father demanded. 'She's never been sick like this before and it happened so fast.'

'That's why we need to do these tests as quickly as possible to find out what's causing it,' Adam stressed. 'If you'll go with Nurse Sullivan, she'll arrange for you to go to a special waiting room and have a drink if you'd like one. I promise I'll come to see you as soon as I have something to tell you.'

'Can't I stay with her, Doctor?' the tearful mother begged. 'She's so little. She's only three—'

'The fewer people there are in here when we do the tests the better. It helps to cut down on the risk of infection,' Adam explained kindly as he shepherded them towards Emma at the door. 'Nurse Sullivan here will be with her when the tests are done so she'll have a friendly face to look at.'

Emma ushered them out of the room and beckoned Dave over, passing on Adam's instructions as she handed the shell-shocked couple into his care. A cryptic explanation was enough to alert him to the serious possibilities without the parents knowing.

'OK. Emma. Here we go,' Adam's brisk voice greeted her as she returned to the room. 'I need one of your best colleagues in here to assist us, and a tray set up for a lumbar puncture as soon as you can.'

Emma sped to do his bidding, her heart going out to the dainty little mite. Within minutes everything was ready, and Janelle was helping to stabilise the little body in position with pillows as Adam approached the trolley. The poor child hadn't made a murmur, submitting drowsily to whatever they wanted.

'Let me just do a final check that her shoulders and hips are vertical to the bed...perfect. Now, Nurse, keep her knees tucked up towards her chest until I tell you to relax them.' Adam glanced across at Emma. 'Alcohol swab and local anaesthetic, please.' He cleaned the skin over the child's lower spine, then held out his hand again for the syringe.

Soon the area between the two vertebrae directly on

the line he'd drawn between the tops of her hips had been numbed and he was able to position the spinal needle.

'Bull's-eye,' he muttered as the cerebrospinal fluid appeared on the first attempt. 'You can let her uncurl slightly now.' And he swiftly transferred about a millilitre of the cloudy liquid into each of the three tubes that Emma had readied.

'Get these up to the lab as soon as possible,' he directed as he completed the procedure. 'One for cultures, one for cell count and the third for chemistries. There's a blood sample to go up at the same time.' He pointed to the tube already on the tray.

Janelle left the room swiftly, with the samples sealed in a marked bag, her mask and gloves discarded carefully just in case they were dealing with a worst-case situation.

'In the meantime, let's get her first dose of intra-venous antibacterial into her.' He turned to find Emma waiting with the prepared syringe and nodded his approval.

Then it was time for her to wrap their little patient up and wait for the results while Adam paid a brief visit to the waiting parents to let them know the tests had been done.

All too soon the results arrived, and he asked Emma to come with him while he broke the bad news to them, leaving Janelle to keep an eye on their patient.

'We've had the results of the tests,' Adam began as

he sat himself in one of the low armchairs. Emma had noticed before that he was careful not to loom over patients. 'I'm afraid Holly's got meningococcal meningitis.'

There was a horrified gasp from the father and his wife collapsed against his shoulder and began to sob.

'Does that mean…?' He paused to gulp. 'Is she going to die?'

'We hope not.' Adam was being careful not to give any guarantees. 'You brought her in as soon as she became ill and we've already started treating her with antibacterial drugs.'

'Can we s-see her?' her red-eyed mother begged.

'Of course you can,' Adam confirmed. 'We're going to have her transferred up to the ward. You'll be able to see her as soon as she's settled, but she'll be in isolation at first.'

'How…how long before we know…?' The poor man couldn't continue.

'Usually the bacteria are cleared from the nose and throat within twenty-four hours of starting treatment, then, providing you follow the guidelines the staff give you, you'll be able to visit her.'

'How did she get it? Where did it come from?' the distraught mother demanded.

'We need to identify any close contacts your daughter has made in the last ten days or so,' Emma said.

'But none of them are ill. We would have heard.'

'Unfortunately, the disease can be passed on by carriers who aren't necessarily sick,' Adam explained. 'In any case, we need to check just in case Holly has infected any of her friends.'

'Oh, God. I didn't think of that.' The woman turned to her husband in horror. 'All those little ones in the play-group…'

'Please don't upset yourself about it at this stage. It will help if you can start making out a list of names while you're waiting to go up to see Holly, then we can begin checking everyone. Any of them who are high-risk will have the chance of vaccination.'

Altogether it was a harrowing morning and Emma was delighted when she came to the end of her shift.

'Half the day left to relax and enjoy yourself,' Dave quipped as she went to retrieve her bag and change her shoes.

'Ha! You mean what's left of the day by the time I do my shopping and lug it home and put it away, then do a load of washing and clean the flat and cook myself a meal!' Emma accused. 'Not all of us have besotted girlfriends to run around after us—or boy-friends, in my case.'

'Just say the word and I'm all yours,' Dave hammed it up.

'No fear,' Emma hooted. 'That would be worse than ever because I'd have you to run round after as well.'

She left him chuckling as she made her way towards the big glass double doors, reaching them at the same time as a certain tall, dark-haired doctor.

'Are you off too?' Emma enquired, then could have bitten her tongue. Talk about asking obvious questions! The man was wearing jeans and a casual shirt and had a leather jacket slung over one broad shoulder, with not a white coat in sight.

'I think they've finally taken pity on me and let me out in time to see something of the area before I'm too tired to focus.' He pulled a wry face. 'All I need now is a guidebook or, better still, a human guide to show me around.' A raised eyebrow punctuated his words to make them almost an invitation.

'I'd be no good, then,' Emma admitted honestly, in spite of the temptation to spend time with him. 'I haven't been in the area long enough to know it well, and I haven't got any transportation to take me outside the town.'

'Well, I've got the transport if you'd be willing to come exploring with me.'

A tiny voice inside her was saying, Yes! Yes! but caution was too much of a habit for her to ignore it so easily.

'I've got all sorts of chores to do—shopping and laundry and—'

'So have I.' He extended one hand in the direction of the glorious summer day in a clear invitation to walk with him. 'You can show me where the best shops are, and when we feel we've done our duty we can play hookey.'

'Hookey?' Emma found herself walking with him

across the car park without a murmur of dissent, almost mesmerised by the fugitive glimmer of gold in his eyes.

'Ah!' he laughed, his teeth starkly white against the bronze of his sun-gilded face, blue-black gleams highlighting the darkness of his hair. 'An Americanism. Go AWOL. Take time out. Skip school…'

Emma nodded her understanding and laughed with him, her heart lifting like a balloon. That's just what it felt like—as if she was taking time out of her life just for herself. Time to spend with the most fascinating man she'd ever met. Time to learn a bit more about him before he disappeared out of her life for good.

It was fun.

For the first time in her life Emma found herself laughing and teasing her way through an afternoon without her old fears intruding.

What was it about Adam Wolf that made her let herself go? If anything, he was the most frightening man she'd ever known. His size and strength set him apart from any of the young men she'd gone out with when she'd still trusted herself enough to go.

Adam was a fully grown adult male in the prime of his life, his virility calling out to everything in her that was female.

Their errands completed, she glanced at him out of the corner of her eye as he strode along beside her, his paces deceptively smooth and silent, almost as if he were a hunting animal stalking his prey…

A shiver that had nothing to do with the fact that the sun had briefly disappeared behind a cloud snaked its way up her spine.

'Cold?'

The question surprised her. She hadn't realised that he was watching her so closely. 'Here's the car. You get inside in the warm. I'll just load up the bags and we'll be on our way.'

He deposited a handful of carrier bags at his feet, and leant forward to unlock the passenger door of the nondescript, mid-range car he'd hired for the duration of his stay in England.

As Emma slid into her seat she still couldn't get over her surprise at his choice of vehicle. Most of the doctors she knew would have chosen something far flashier, far more impressive, especially if they were single men on the loose in a foreign country.

Adam was different, though, she conceded as she obeyed his reminder to fasten her seat belt. He had no need of expensive cars to bolster his self-esteem. He seemed to be the most completely self-contained man she'd ever met, both in his work at the hospital, which was superb, and in his private life.

As far as she could tell from the hospital grapevine, he hadn't accepted a single one of the invitations he'd received—no matter how blatant. And yet he'd suggested spending an afternoon with her, shopping and doing their laundry, for all the world as if they were an old married couple.

The warm glow this thought started deep inside her

was doused by a counterbalancing one, which reminded her spitefully that she obviously wasn't interesting enough to take on a proper date...

'Can I leave my laundry here until I bring you back later?' His deep voice broke into her musings as he drew up outside the drab building containing her minute flat.

'Later?' What was he talking about? she asked herself. Where was he going now?

'When we come back from our voyage of exploration,' he explained as if she were simple. 'Don't tell me you've forgotten!'

That smile! Emma blinked. Much more of it and she'd be forgetting her own name.

'But...'

'But nothing! A promise is a promise. You can't expect me to find my way around when I'm having to drive on the wrong side of the road...and there's all that food to eat! Get yourself inside that house quick and dump everything. Time's wasting!'

Emma laughed and tumbled out of the car. This was a new side to the solemn Dr Wolf—an exuberance for life that was utterly contagious. She took most of the bags from the back seat.

'Back in ten minutes,' she flung over her shoulder with a smile.

'Never happen,' he taunted. 'No woman is capable of taking less than half an hour.' He slid himself down in his seat as though preparing himself for a long wait.

Emma blessed him for his tactfulness in staying in

the car as she grabbed her belongings and sped inside. Her tiny rooms would never have coped with his overwhelming presence, especially as she would be trying to put her shopping away and change her clothes at the same time.

Nine minutes later Emma was still panting with the exertion of proving him wrong as she approached the car.

'OK, smart-ass! Apologise!' she demanded in an atrocious imitation of his accent as she stuck her arm through the open window to display her watch under his nose. 'Nine minutes!'

She leant forward to watch the expression on his face in the shadowed interior of the car, the hair she'd released from its professional-looking imprisonment tumbling forward over her shoulder to caress the side of her face.

Dark eyes gleamed at her from between slitted lids, then he moved suddenly to trap her wrist in fingers of steel, and before she could take evasive action he'd leant forward to plant a peck on the parted softness of her lingering, triumphant smile.

'Good. Hop in,' he ordered as calmly as if the sparks of electricity which had crackled over her lips at the contact had never happened.

Emma was silent as she sat beside him, her hand cradled over the warmth which lingered in her wrist where he had held her. She was lost for words after his totally unexpected action as he started the engine and pulled out into the traffic.

'Hey!'

The tone of his deep voice told her that it wasn't the first time he'd tried to attract her attention.

'Earth to Emma! Earth to Emma! Tell me which direction to take before we get to the end of this road or I might end up going round in circles!'

Jerked out of her daydream, Emma laughed at his nonsense and spread the large-scale map over her jeans-clad knees.

'Which way do you want to go? Is there anywhere in particular you want to visit?'

'Surprise me!' he invited with a grin. 'This is my first time in England, the sun is shining and there's a beautiful girl in the car with me. Anything else is a bonus!'

'Ha!' Outwardly Emma scorned his flattery and set about giving him directions, but inside, where there had been no sunshine for years, a little seed had tentatively started to germinate.

'I know what's so different!' Adam's voice was filled with the enthusiasm of discovery after nearly an hour of meandering around the highways and byways to the north of the town where St Lawrence's was situated.

They'd crossed over the motorway soon after setting out and had caught sight of the build-up of holiday traffic going towards the West Country, but soon she'd directed him into the more rural areas, sending him down some turnings just because they liked the sound of the names of the villages.

'Different about what?' Emma demanded.

'Different about England,' he clarified. 'The horizon is much closer than it is back home.'

'It would be. You're driving down a lane surrounded by hedges,' Emma scoffed. 'I don't suppose the horizon is very far away in New York when you're surrounded by skyscrapers either.'

'*Touché*!' he conceded. 'But if you'd ever seen Montana, you'd know what I mean.'

'Is Montana near Seattle?'

'Hardly!' Adam laughed indulgently. 'It's about four hundred and fifty miles as the crow flies, with a mountain range in between!'

'Oh.' Emma felt the heat in her cheeks at her ignorance.

'Don't sweat it.' There was still a chuckle in his voice. 'I've made some major blunders too, like asking Alec MacTavish what part of England he was from!'

'Oh, Lord, you didn't,' she chuckled.

'Then I made the mistake of calling him Scotch instead of Scots, and had a five-minute dressing down in the middle of Reception.'

'"Ye dr-r-rink Scotch, mon!"' Emma quoted wickedly. 'I've heard that speech several times in the last couple of years.'

'It certainly makes sure you never make that mistake again,' Adam agreed. 'But I noticed he didn't invite me to partake of any of it to fix it in my memory!'

Soon after that his stomach started rumbling and

they found a small patch of woodland for their im-
promptu picnic, the beech trees sounding almost like
distant waves as the breeze rustled its way through
them.

Unfortunately the light began to fade long before
Emma was ready for the day to end, and she found
herself moving slower and slower as they packed everything away into the car.

Finally it was time to climb back inside and, once
seated, she twisted to locate the seat-belt point.

'Emma?' His hand settled over hers, preventing her
from pushing the latch home, and she looked up to
meet eyes gleaming darkly in the shadows. 'I hope
you've enjoyed this as much as I have?'

The strange uncertainty in his voice barely registered in her brain through the overload of emotion that
she was picking up through their physical contact.

Attraction.

Never had she been so aware of another person's
reaction to her. 'Yes,' she whispered, totally overwhelmed. She didn't really know whether she was
agreeing to her enjoyment of their afternoon together
or to her own answering fascination with him.

For long moments they were still, gazing into each
other's eyes in taut silence while a strange connection
seemed to weave itself between them.

'Good,' Adam murmured in a husky voice as he
finally released her hand. 'That's good.' He gave a
decisive nod as he turned back to secure his own
seat belt.

* * *

By the time he drew up outside her flat again it was
completely dark, only the intermittent circles of yellow
streetlights showing her where she lived.

'Hang on a second.' Adam released his belt at the
same time. 'I'll come with you to get my bags.'

'Don't bother. I'll bring them out to you.' Emma's
offer was ignored.

'No way, lady,' he drawled decisively as he unfolded his long legs and straightened up out of the car.
'At this time of night, I see my date safely to her door.'

A burst of raucous laughter punctuated his words
even as Emma was basking in the delight of being
called his date, and a ragtag bunch of youths spilled
out of an untidy house further up the road.

Adam had moved round to escort Emma across the
road by the time the group reached them.

'Hey, man. Look. It's a hippy,' one called, brave in
the company of his friends. 'What you doin' this side
of town?'

Adam angled his body so that Emma was protected
behind him and straightened himself to his full height.

'You hear me?' The noisy youth strutted like a ban-
tam rooster, with his coterie around him. 'I'm talking
to you.'

Adam stayed silent, his hands hanging easily by his
sides as he watched the group coming closer, egging
each other on.

As Emma maintained a watchful position just behind him she knew that there was little danger of vi-

olence—Adam wouldn't let it happen while she was in his care.

The rowdy group only grew quiet when they realised that their target was totally unimpressed by them. Only *then* did they seem to recognise just how tall he was, how broad and powerful his shoulders were and how menacing he was in his utter stillness and silence.

Emma was aware of the moment when their puny nerve broke in the face of his sheer presence, and she could have laughed aloud at the panic-filled thoughts that she was picking up from them.

'Adam?' she murmured as the group finally slunk off, content with mouthing a barrage of insults once they were well out of reach. 'Shall I get your laundry?'

His chuckle came from deep inside his chest. 'I don't know if that's going from the sublime to the ridiculous or the other way round, but lead on.' And he finally ushered her over the road.

Emma fumbled for her key, suddenly far more nervous at the prospect of having Adam Wolf in the intimacy of her flat than she'd been of that group of miscreants a few minutes ago.

She swung the door open and switched the light on in the communal hallway as she entered, the hairs on the back of her neck telling her that he was following her inside.

'I'll wait here while you get my things,' he murmured, and she glanced back sharply to see him lean easily back against the wall and fold his arms across the impressive width of his chest.

With a muttered agreement, Emma flew up the stairs to her own rooms, her heart beating with a mixture of relief at the unexpected reprieve and disappointment that Adam hadn't been willing to come up with her.

'There you are.' She held out two bags of laundry as she rejoined him moments later. 'I'll see you in A and E tomorrow,' she said brightly, proud of the casual way in which she was dealing with the situation.

Adam turned towards the door as if to leave, then bent down to deposit the bags against the wall before he resumed his original position, the leather of his jacket creaking as he folded his arms again.

'You were very calm out there.' He angled his head towards the road.

'I knew nothing would happen,' she said with calm conviction.

'Why? Do they do that sort of thing often?'

'No, it was the first time.'

'Then how…?'

'I knew you wouldn't let anything happen.' Her voice was only just louder than a whisper but it shouted her belief in him.

'Emma,' he groaned as he shouldered himself away from the wall and captured her hands to pull her into his arms.

CHAPTER FOUR

'Nurse!'

The call had more than a hint of panic in it and Emma responded swiftly.

'Yes? What can I—? Ah! I see!' The reason for the receptionist's urgency was evident as the young man in front of her doubled over again to be sick on the floor.

'Please, Mr Retallack, will you go with Nurse Sullivan?' Poor Mrs Burton sounded less than her usual unflappable self.

'Ring through to Custodial and get them to send someone straight up,' Emma reminded her, with a wry smile as she put her arm around the man's shoulders and led her distressed charge away.

'How long have you been like this, Mr Retallack?' Emma began her questions as soon as she'd provided him with a bowl.

'Coupla days,' he answered, his forehead dotted with sweat and his skin almost grey under the bright lights.

'Do you know what brought it on?' She took a chance and handed him a thermometer as soon as he was sitting.

'Thought it were eitherways food poisoning or stummick bug.' He closed pale lips around the cylinder, robbing Emma of her chance to hear any more of his wonderful accent.

When she retrieved it and confirmed her suspicions she handed him over to Penny. 'Will you help Mr Retallack to take his clothes off if he can't manage alone, and then get him up on the table? I'll get the doctor to come and have a look at him.' She shut the door behind her and went in search of Adam.

'Mrs Burton? Do you know where Dr Wolf is?'

'He was on his way to Emergency Room One last time I saw him.' She smiled wanly at Emma as she presided over her newly cleaned domain. 'Sorry about the panic just then, but I thought it was going all over the desk any minute.'

'No problem,' Emma consoled her. 'Thank God for the custodial staff!'

'Hear, hear!' the older woman muttered with feeling as Emma took herself off down the opposite corridor.

She'd almost reached the double doors to Emergency Room One when they were pushed open by a trolley.

'Coming through,' a warning voice called, and she stepped nimbly aside. 'Grab the lift, will you, Emma? Going up to Theatre Four.' Dave was following the trolley with an armful of notes and X-ray plates.

Emma reached out to thumb the button and the arrow lit up. 'On its way,' she confirmed, and continued on her quest for Adam Wolf, holding one of the doors open to enter the room after the trolley was clear.

His back was towards her as the door swished closed behind her, his head bent forward as he concentrated on the voice on the telephone.

'Right.' His deep voice broke the quiet of the room. 'He should be with you in a couple of minutes. Good luck—I've a feeling you're going to need it with that one.' And he returned the receiver to the cradle.

He turned to face the room with a concerned frown etched between his dark eyebrows, his mind obviously still on the patient he'd been talking about.

She had taken two steps towards him before her presence broke his concentration.

'Emma,' he said softly, and stood still, his expression almost wary.

'Adam.' She smiled, her pulse throbbing at the base of her throat as she fought the memory of the moments she'd spent in his arms.

'Were you looking for me?'

His voice had the same husky timbre as it had when he'd buried his face in the profusion of her unbound hair and she'd had to fight the impulse to launch herself towards him and wrap her arms around the taut muscles of his waist.

'Oh! Yes!' His words finally penetrated the haze of memories. 'Can you come and take a look at a young man for me? His blood pressure's ninety over sixty, pulse ninety-nine between bouts of vomiting, respiration similarly variable. Rebound tenderness on the right. He thought it was food poisoning or a stomach bug, but I'm certain it's appendicitis and I've a feeling that it's just about to go—'

Before she'd finished speaking he was on the move, his long legs covering the ground effortlessly so that Emma had to work hard to keep up.

'Is he constipated or has he got diarrhoea? Did you manage to get a urine sample? When did he last have anything to eat or drink?' The questions were thrown towards her one after the other.

'Severe diarrhoea and pain on urinating, but he managed a sample and I took blood as well. He hasn't had anything since yesterday evening.' She answered each question in order, her brisk tone an exact copy of his own.

'Good.' His eyes met hers briefly as he turned to shoulder the door open, and he lowered one eyelid in an intimate wink. 'Let's see what we've got.' And he was all businesslike again as he reached for the container of examining gloves.

In a very short space of time Mr Retallack was on his way up in the lift, with a surgeon waiting at the other end of the short journey ready to perform an emergency appendectomy.

'Well spotted,' Adam praised and he stripped off his gloves and disposed of them. 'If they get moving upstairs, they should get it out without it perforating.'

'Either way, he's out of our hands now.' She

glanced up at the clock on the wall. 'I'll just go and check what else has come in, otherwise you might have time to get a pot of coffee going.' She gave him a cheeky grin as she left the room.

'You're very pally with the hunk,' a sharp voice commented as the door closed behind her, and Emma turned to see Marilyn Venning coming out of the opposite door. 'Organising private coffee-breaks with him now, are we?'

'Oh, yes,' Emma agreed, with a bland expression. 'So private that the whole A and E can walk in at any time.' She just had time to see the slyly calculating look on the tall, voluptuous blonde's face when the doors burst open behind her.

'Emma, I need you.' Adam's voice was urgent and Emma's heart performed a spectacular double somersault in her chest as she heard Marilyn's gasp. 'There's been a major crash on the motorway,' he continued before she had time to embarrass herself.

'They need the team from St Lawrence's to attend and I was told you've been trained for it.'

'That's quite right.' All of a sudden Marilyn's pettiness was forgotten as she switched her brain into top gear.

'Equipment's kept ready, packed and labelled.' She took off in the direction of the ambulance embarkation point. 'Protective clothing's on board and we have radio contact and telemetry for transmitting electrocardiograms back to the hospital from the site of the accident.'

'Gotcha.' He raised a thumb as, with the rest of the group, they reached the vehicles. 'Give me a shove if I'm not where I should be.' His breathing was hardly altered by their dash along the corridor and Emma consoled herself with the fact that his legs were a great deal longer than hers—something he was proving as he tried to fold them as small as possible into a space between the packages of equipment.

'Hang onto your hats,' the driver called as he accelerated out of the bay, delaying switching on his siren only just long enough to avoid deafening them in the enclosed area.

He swung the vehicle into a tight turn and Emma slid across the seat, to land plastered against Adam's side, the Citroën pulling away with a speed that still astonished her every time.

Her face grew warm as she shuffled until they were separated by a couple of inches, but the seat belt wasn't sufficient to prevent her from sliding just as helplessly as they negotiated a roundabout before they reached the road onto the motorway.

'Might as well stay put and save your energy,' Adam murmured in her ear as he secured his arm around her shoulders. Then he raised his voice for the benefit of the two in front. 'I think our driver moonlights as a stunt man.'

There was a burst of appreciative laughter from the

front seat. 'Nah! Far too tame after ambulance driving,' he boasted. 'This baby will cruise at a hundred and thirty miles an hour and still have enough under the bonnet for a burst of real speed.'

The radio broke in with some rapid conversation demanding their estimated time of arrival at the crash, the voice on the other end sounding as unflustered as if the whole thing was a practice exercise.

'ETA four minutes,' the driver, named Don, confirmed. 'One doctor, one nurse and two paramedics on board.'

'Is that usual?' Adam blinked when he heard the level of qualification of the other two in the vehicle.

'For *this* team, yes,' Emma said. 'Being so close to a major motorway we need to have access to the best in a hurry. As the personnel have to be able to double for each other in a lot of situations, it makes sense if the driver can work when he gets there, too.'

'Logical,' Adam agreed, with a nod. 'It sounds as if the situation in the UK is developing in a similar way to the USA. Thirty years ago there weren't any paramedics; now there are over fifty thousand.'

'Ah, but did you know that Belfast, in Northern Ireland, was one of the first places in the world to have the forerunners of the paramedics?' Emma challenged. 'We don't just copy American ideas, we're willing to pick up on anything worthwhile—'

'Here we go!' Don's voice broke in from the front

seat and their eyes were drawn to the front windscreen and the terrible scene that met them.

The whole area was cordoned off by police and other emergency vehicles, their flashing warning lights incongruous on such a beautiful, sunny day.

The ambulance was directed to the side of the road. By the time the vehicle drew to a halt all four doors were open and the team was exiting as fast as they could as voices and arms waved to them to hurry in several different directions, each one wanting their attention first.

'Lorry driver trapped…'

'Injured children in the car…'

'Motorcyclist…'

Emma was trying to look in all directions at once.

'Where do we start?' she said, horrified at the carnage surrounding them.

'With the first one we come to, in the absence of any other directions,' Don said through gritted teeth as he swung a pack of supplies out. 'I hope to God someone here knows what they're doing and has started triage.' And he was away.

'Doctor!' A policeman was waving in their direction, obviously catching sight of the fluorescent markings on Adam's vest.

'What have you got?' Adam demanded as he reached the knot of rescuers, his bag gripped firmly in one gloved hand.

'You'd better have a look at him in the cab. He's

losing a hell of a lot of blood. At this rate he'll run out before we can cut him out. We put a collar on him and he's got oxygen…'

It was a good job that Adam had long legs, Emma thought as she held his bag while he climbed carefully up the side of the shattered cab of the articulated lorry.

'Hey, man,' he said calmly as he reached in to make contact with the trapped driver, 'any room in there for another one?'

'Oh, God,' Emma heard the unseen man groan. 'Not another bloody American hitchhiker!'

There were several seconds of startled silence before Adam burst into full-throated laughter, the sound odd amid such carnage. 'I take it that's an example of never-say-die British humour,' he chuckled as he manoeuvred gingerly to assess the extent of the man's injuries.

'Emma,' he called back over his shoulder, 'I need to get a temporary tourniquet above this while I sort out how to get a pressure bandage on it. If I had another pair of hands, I'd also put up an IV to start replacing lost fluids.'

'Coming right up,' Emma confirmed as she tapped the back of her hand against his leg, and he extended an arm back to have the items he'd requested placed straight in his hand without having to turn round.

'Dammit, I need to be an octopus,' he was muttering as he struggled to position the flat folds of triangular bandage as a torniquet and tighten it effectively at the same time.

'Will two more hands do on loan until you can have the grafts done for the rest?' Emma queried as she reached across from the other side of the cab to hold it in place.

'Emma?' He was frowning fiercely as their eyes clashed across the driver's body. 'What the hell are you doing in here?'

'My job,' she said sweetly, leaving him to continue his task as she tied a length of soft rubber tubing around the man's arm, swabbed the good, strong vein it raised and smoothly inserted the needle attached to the prepared macrodrop infusion set.

'I'll just get rid of my torniquet, and tape this lot in position—' Emma was suiting her actions to her words '—then you can tell me where you need my hands.'

There was a choking sound from the driver and they both looked sharply at him to find that he was trying to stifle laughter. 'Doc, that was an offer you can't refuse!'

'Oh, yes, I can.' Adam smiled at their plucky patient. 'If I take her up on that sort of offer, it won't be in front of an audience!'

'*If*? What do you mean, *if*? Haven't you Yanks got any red blood in your veins?' he demanded, his voice gradually growing shakier.

'Quite a bit more than you have at this moment, so

stop shouting the odds,' Emma scolded, her face still fiery from her realisation of her verbal gaffe. 'It's not a good idea to start insulting the man who's trying to stop you bleeding all over the place.'

'Sorry, Nurse,' he said, his voice apparently meek, but Emma saw the twinkle in his eyes and the wink he gave her when Adam looked away.

Between the two of them Emma and Adam had managed to apply direct pressure over the site of greatest bleeding just in time for the fire brigade team to take over.

They could safely leave him now that he was stabilised, knowing that the heavy-duty equipment would make short work of the structure of the cab and release the driver. After that, he would be loaded into one of the ambulances which were ferrying the injured off to hospital.

They both jumped clear of the wrecked lorry and hurried in the direction of a motorcyclist lying between two cars.

In the few seconds it took for his long legs to eat up the distance, Adam's eyes were focusing on one damaged vehicle after another, checking to see how many people were still in need of help.

'It looks as if all the minor injuries have gone,' Emma said after her own rapid survey of the scene. 'This is probably the last of the bad ones, as far as I can see.'

Their second patient was still unconscious, and after

they'd confirmed that his condition hadn't deteriorated since the initial taking of his vital signs it was decided that, once he was immobilised on a backboard, it would be better if he was transported to hospital for further investigation.

'Before we can touch him, we've got to stabilise his neck,' Adam muttered as he struggled to place the neck brace without disturbing the man's position.

'It wouldn't take me a second to get that helmet out of your way.' The helpful voice was accompanied by a pair of hands which were already reaching towards the brightly coloured dome.

'Don't you dare!' Emma's forceful voice rang out before Adam had a chance to speak, and the advancing hands froze instantly. 'I've actually seen a patient whose skull was shattered when he hit the road, and the only thing that was holding it together was the helmet. He walked away from the accident only to be killed by a helpful friend who pulled his helmet off.'

'Oh, God!' The young man's face turned quite green and Emma knew that that was one message he would never forget.

'Effective,' Adam muttered under his breath as they assisted in the young man's transfer to a backboard.

'It also happens to be true,' she replied softly. 'He tried to make a date with my friend in Casualty while he was waiting to be seen by the doctor, and five minutes later he was dead.'

'Rough,' Adam murmured, the single word conveying all that was needed.

'Doc! Quick!'

Adam's head went up as he tried to locate the caller amongst the noises and shouts all around them.

'Here, Doc!' Several arms waved him over towards the car and towing caravan at the heart of the tragedy.

Adam spared a last, quick glance at the deeply unconscious motorcyclist before he grabbed his bag to lope swiftly away. He knew as well as Emma did that the waiting ambulance crew were well able to take care of the man from this point until he reached hospital.

'What have you got?' he demanded as he reached the knot of rescuers.

'We've found another one…'

'We thought we'd got them all…'

'When the woman came to…'

Several voices broke in as one burly fireman, who'd been hunched down on the ground, turned awkwardly to reveal the tiny bundle, cradled in his huge hands as carefully as a piece of priceless Meissen china. Emma recognised what he was holding just as she was assailed by the agonising feeling of loss that she was picking up from Adam.

She watched silently as he dropped to his knees without a word and began checking the fragile burden, then she crouched down beside him, poised to supply whatever he needed.

'We didn't realise there was a baby in the car until the mother regained consciousness.' The many voices had resolved themselves into one spokesman. 'The driver was dead on impact and she was out cold. There was no safety seat so we had no reason to look. The baby must have been on her lap when it happened, and he ended up in the footwell under the dashboard. He hasn't moved or made a sound since we found him.'

The speaker was a seasoned veteran of many such scenes, but even *he* was unable to keep an emotional tone out of his voice.

There was a pause while the surrounding men almost seemed to hold their breath as they watched Adam checking the baby's vital signs.

'Is he going to be all right?' One man finally voiced the question on all their faces.

'I don't know.' Adam raised his eyes briefly from his task. 'He's had a blow to the side of his head and we won't know how much damage it's done until we do some more tests.'

Emma helped him start the IV line, the two of them simultaneously muttering imprecations under their breath as they searched for a vein big enough. Positioning an oxygen supply was just as precarious, and when they finally had everything regulated to his satisfaction Adam looked up at their audience, frowning darkly. 'Where's the mother?'

'In the ambulance.' A hand pointed. 'She nearly

went mental when we took her away. Refused to be
taken to hospital till we got the baby out. Will you
travel back with them?'

'Unless you've got anything else?' Adam's words
were clipped. The fact that the rich depth was missing
from his voice was Emma's clue that he was searingly
angry. It was to his credit that he didn't allow it to
spill over into his dealings with other people.

'Well, thanks for your help with this lot. No doubt
we'll be seeing you again at some stage.'

The rescue co-ordinator's words were following
them across the intervening space as Adam gently bore
the limp scrap of humanity away, Emma bringing up
the rear with his hastily gathered bag of belongings.

'My baby! Did you save my baby…?'

Emma saw Adam's assessing glance go over the
woman, noting her pale, shocked appearance and the
angry knot on the side of her forehead, the collar that
was protecting her neck making her movements awkward.

'We've got him out, and he's still alive—at the moment,' he said curtly, and Emma gasped audibly as the
baby's mother reeled back and nearly passed out, only
Emma's quick reflexes saving her from crumpling in
a heap on the floor of the ambulance.

'Doctor,' she muttered with as much indignation in
the word as she dared, her hand anchoring the
woman's elbow while she straightened.

'Oh, God, he can't die,' the shaky voice rose in a wail. 'He mustn't die—I couldn't bear it!'

Emma reached for her again, this time her arm going around the slender shoulders as they shook with racking sobs.

'Shh now. Shh!' she soothed, glaring at Adam's stony face. 'You won't do the baby any good with this noise. What's his name?'

'A-Adam,' she choked, and sniffed. 'I called him Adam because it's a strong name. I thought it would help him when he grew up if he had a strong name. Do you think it helps?' She raised pink eyelids in appeal to Emma.

'Perhaps you should ask the doctor.' Emma turned to their silently brooding companion with a militant expression in her eyes. 'By sheer coincidence, his name's Adam too. He can tell you if it's made him strong.'

There was a long silence following Emma's pronouncement as the distraught woman turned her gaze to the powerful man holding her tiny baby.

'I don't know.' When the words came, his voice sounded almost rusty. 'I think we have to make the best of what we're given and just keep trying—' He stopped suddenly, his eyes flying to the tiny bundle, held so securely in his arms despite the fact that the ambulance was now travelling at full speed towards the hospital.

'He moved.' Emma saw his lips form the words and

saw, too, the glimmer of hope in his eyes when he looked at her. 'I felt him move and his eyelids just flickered...'

Emma felt the burst of uncontrollable emotions in him: wonder, caring, protectiveness...anger.

'If you love him so much, why didn't you take care of him?' he accused the cowering woman, his voice filled with anguish. 'Why wasn't he strapped in a car-seat, safe in the back? Surely you knew that he shouldn't have been on your lap?'

Emma's arm was still wrapped supportively round the woman's shoulders, helping to brace her against the motion of the speeding vehicle, and she felt her slight frame stiffen; felt, too, her inner hurt at Adam's totally unexpected attack *and* sensed the second when it turned to rage.

'Yes, Doctor,' she grated through clenched teeth, 'I *do* know that he should have been in a safety seat, but *unfortunately* he arrived earlier than we expected and, instead of getting all that sorted out, my *husband* spent the week I was in hospital catching up with all his old drinking pals.

'Of course,' she continued relentlessly, 'the fact that we had a tiny baby didn't make *any* difference to the plans he'd made for his annual holiday, nor was he willing to stop at the services while I fed him, in spite of the fact that he started off this morning with a hang-over and refused to admit he was falling asleep at the wheel...

'Oh, the bastard—the rotten, selfish bastard,' she wailed. 'If my baby dies, I'll kill him. I'll kill him with my own hands. It's all his fault. All his bloody fault…'

She finally ran out of words and breath and sat there, her eyes fixed on her infant son, ignoring the twin streams which flowed silently down her cheeks.

Horrified, Emma suddenly realised that the poor woman still didn't know what had happened to her husband. Her eyes flew to Adam's face and saw the same shocked expression as she knew was on hers.

Before she could think of a way they could break the news, they were drawing up outside the hospital and the opportunity was lost.

There was nearly another fight when Adam started to stride down the corridor with the unconscious child in his arms. The ambulance man who was carrying the IV bag and oxygen cylinder was almost having to run to keep up with him, and Head Nurse Noone stepped in to catch hold of the tiny child's mother to stop her following them through to the restricted area.

'No. Let me go.' She was tugging against the firm hold on her elbow. 'You can't stop me—'

'Please,' Emma intervened gently, and rested her hand casually on the woman's arm to make the important contact. 'You were knocked unconscious in the crash. You need to be checked over to make sure you're going to be all right.'

'But he's taking my baby away. I want to go with my baby.' Her tear-reddened eyes were full of fear.

'I promise you, Dr Wolf will be taking very good care of him.' Emma concentrated on projecting calm through her touch. 'He's hardly likely to do less than his best for someone who shares the same name…'

The attempt at humour raised a weak excuse for a smile, but the mother seemed calmer and finally submitted to an examination after she was promised that she could join her baby as soon as the paediatrician had seen him.

While she was being taken to a cubicle, Emma rapidly explained the circumstances to Barbara Noone so that she could pass them on to the senior registrar who would be seeing the woman.

Someone, somewhere along the line, was going to have to tell the poor woman that her husband had died in the crash.

'I'm just glad it's not part of *my* job,' Emma said that lunchtime, when she actually managed to reach the canteen for a snatched meal and ended up sitting with one of the junior nurses from Paediatrics.

'We still end up sitting in on enough of those types of interviews, though,' a charge nurse from Orthopaedics commented. 'We might not be the ones actually doing the telling, but we usually get left to do the mopping up when the big noises have gone.'

There was a general murmur of agreement.

'Perhaps…?' Emma paused in her train of thought.

'What?' the junior prompted.

'Well, I was thinking that perhaps we get the fallout because the patients or their relatives see more of us and feel they know us that much better.'

'You mean they know us well enough to be rude to us?' The charge nurse pulled a face.

'Maybe that's part of it,' Emma said thoughtfully, 'but I think it's more a case that they feel they can trust us because they see us doing our best for them hour by hour, and they know we'll understand what they're going through.'

'Hey, Emma.' A staff nurse she recognised from Obstetrics and Gynaecology muttered an aside across the table. 'Do you know a tall, dark-haired dreamboat with the most fabulous eyes? Because there's one at the table behind you who's hardly taken them off you since he sat down.'

Emma felt the heat steal up her throat and into her cheeks but refused to turn around and give rise to any gossip—the rumour mill in the hospital was bad enough without her providing any grist.

She'd known that he was there, of course. Her private radar had told her as soon as he'd entered the room, the prickle of awareness sending a shiver up her spine and raising the soft hairs on the back of her neck.

It had been her sense of self-preservation that had made her concentrate on her conversation with her colleagues around the table. Inside, every nerve in her body was screaming with the knowledge that he was looking at her, the touch of his eyes almost as tangible as a physical caress.

'You must be imagining it,' she murmured uncomfortably, wondering what on earth Adam would think if he realised that he was a target for such speculation.

Several people left the table, their allotted breaks over, and Emma silently sighed with relief. The fewer people who heard this conversation the better, she thought as her tormentor leaned towards her with a sly grin.

'You wait and see,' she said confidently. 'This one looks like the ultimate predator—a bona fide wolf in wolf's clothing. I think he's just sitting there biding his time until we've all gone so he can move in for the kill. Even *you* won't be immune to this one... Oh!'

'What's the matter?' Emma tried to sound innocent but she was struggling to control a smile.

'He's going!' The nurse sounded quite disappointed.

'Told you so. ' Emma knew that she sounded disgustingly smug, but the temptation to say it was too much to resist, especially as her sensitivity to his presence had let her know that he was going before her companion had told her.

'Darn.' The grin was wry. 'I was really hoping I was going to be in on the start of some fresh gossip to liven up the tedium of bedpan time. Ah, well,' she sighed theatrically, and took her tray over to the collection point, waggling her fingers in a brief farewell before she left the canteen.

Emma lifted her coffee-cup and cradled it in front of her face between both hands to hide her smile.

'Is the coast clear?' Adam's deep voice murmured from behind her. 'Can I lure you away from the delights of the staff canteen with the promise of a mug of my *real* coffee?'

CHAPTER FIVE

'FOR a mug of *real* coffee, I'd follow you to the ends of the earth—or at least to the end of the corridor in A and E!' Emma laughed up at Adam as the cup of grey liquid she'd been cradling in her hands was deposited with the rest of the debris on her tray.

She couldn't help chuckling as he struck his head out of the canteen door and ostentatiously looked each way with a shifty expression on his face.

'The coast is clear,' he hissed.

'I'm not afraid of being seen with you,' Emma hastened to assure him, momentarily worried that he might still harbour doubts about her feelings on that score.

'Ah, but if no one sees me spirit you away to my lair they won't know the wolf has you in his clutches.' He grinned a mock-predatory smile, his teeth gleaming whitely under the fluorescent lights of the corridor.

'Idiot,' Emma scolded. 'I gathered you'd heard what she was saying when you left the canteen.'

'We wolves have very sharp hearing,' he confirmed before his expression grew serious. 'Is it going to be a problem for you if people start linking us together? Will it put anyone's nose out of joint?'

'Yes,' Emma confirmed in a suitably grave tone, and felt a swift dart of satisfaction at the momentary disappointment which crossed his face. 'I'll probably get hate mail from every nurse in the place for attracting the attention of the dishiest doctor in the hospital.'

She was amazed to see the tide of red staining the high planes of his cheeks as he muttered an embarrassed disclaimer and hurried across the room to busy himself with the gadget in the corner, which was sending out its tantalising aroma.

'Adam?' Emma began tentatively when they were finally sitting down in adjoining chairs. 'There's something…' She paused, not knowing quite how to continue. All she did know was that it was important for her own peace of mind.

'What?' His eyes were shielded by thick dark lashes as he gazed fixedly at the mug between his hands.

'That can't possibly be the first time someone's paid you a compliment.' Her words sounded almost like an accusation. 'With looks like yours, you must have had women queueing up since you were in your teens.'

The color returned to his face, darker than ever.

'Of course,' he agreed baldly, his eyes fixed on hers with a cold anger. 'Unfortunately, most of them viewed me as something in the line of an exotic pet—something to be displayed as some sort of trophy until the novelty wore off, when I would be discarded for a new toy.'

Emma had suffered from that once or twice herself

and knew what it felt like. 'They don't realise how demeaning it is to be valued just for your entertainment value rather than as a person,' she murmured almost under her breath.

There was a moment of startled silence before he spoke again. 'I didn't think you'd understand—didn't think anyone who wasn't handicapped in some way—physically, mentally or by their religion or colour—would understand what it feels like.' There was a new respect in his eyes.

'Not all handicaps are that easy to spot,' she muttered as the warmth of his approval melted a little of the ice deep inside where she kept her own emotions.

Suddenly, she remembered their last tiny patient at the site of the crash.

'How's your little namesake doing? What did Paediatrics have to say?'

'"Wait and see."' He pressed his lips together in an impatient line. 'Poor little guy. He's less than two weeks old and he could end up brain-damaged or even dead because his parents didn't care enough to make sure he was safe.'

'That's not fair,' Emma objected, stung by his blanket condemnation. 'His mother cares.'

'Not enough to insist that her child's properly taken care of,' he insisted. 'So much for mother love.'

'You're very quick to set yourself up as judge and jury, aren't you? Everything's so cut and dried, isn't it?' she scorned. 'The baby should have been taken care of, and she's the mother so it was her job to take care of it—in spite of the fact that she had a Caesarean delivery less than two weeks ago and her doctor told her she shouldn't be going away, in spite of the fact that she was only five feet two and weighed less than a hundred pounds, wet through, and was married to a rugby-playing, hard-drinking man of six feet who weighed twice what she did. It was his baby too!' She was almost panting for breath by the time she reached the end.

'Point taken,' Adam said quietly into the fraught silence which stretched between them, his dark eyes thoughtful as they rested on her heated face. 'But I doubt you'd have allowed it to happen to a child of yours, even if you were married to Goliath.'

Emma was heartened by the implied compliment. 'I would hope that whomever I chose to be the father of my child would love and care for him as much as I did,' she said, and was swept by a wave of mingled anger and pain emanating from the self-contained man who refused to let any trace of either emotion show on his face.

Someone had hurt Adam Wolf.

At some time in his past someone—probably a woman—had hurt him so deeply that his respect for women as a whole had been all but destroyed.

She found herself idly imagining what a child of his would look like, and was captivated by the mental image of a solemn-faced miniature of that handsome face, the lean planes softened by baby chubbiness.

A sad longing filled her that she would never know if she was right. The tentative friendship they were building was unlikely to last long after he returned to the other side of the world and got caught up in his own busy life.

Still, she thought, briskly banishing impossible dreams which had her cradling the tiny dark-eyed child to her own breast, he was here for three months, and at least she would have the memories of his friendship to look back on when he left.

'Back to work.' She glanced up at the clock and pushed herself to her feet. 'I'm amazed it's been quiet as long as this. Thanks for the coffee.' She saluted him with her cup as she took it over to the sink to rinse it out.

'Emma?'

For a minute she wasn't sure whether she'd heard the softly spoken word or imagined it.

'Yes?' She leant back against the edge of the sink unit and clasped her hands together.

'Will you…?' He paused and gave his head a slight shake. 'Have you ever ridden a horse?'

'Yes,' she replied hesitantly. 'But I haven't been riding for years, since I was a child.' She shrugged.

'If your day off is still tomorrow, would you come with me?' He seemed to have come to an important decision, his words firm and deliberate.

'Come where?' Emma sidestepped her immediate impulse to agree to anything as long as it was in his company. She couldn't afford the heartbreak that could bring.

'I saw an advertisement for some stables a few miles outside town, where you can hire horses by the hour. Would you like to come?'

'Yes, I'd love to,' she managed calmly while her heart was turning cartwheels round her chest.

'Great.' He threw her one of those lethal smiles and she began to wonder if her pulse would ever be normal around him. 'I'll pick you up about ten tomorrow.'

'No!' she yelped. 'I've got a load of laundry and an empty fridge to fill before I can go gallivanting off on horseback. If I don't do some chores I'll end up having to wipe my feet as I come *out* of the house, it'll be so dirty.'

'OK,' he conceded, with a nod. 'You shovel out the mess and I'll arrive at ten to take you shopping. Then we can set off as soon as we've stacked it in your fridge.'

It was an order rather than a suggestion but Emma hadn't the heart to point that out; the boyishly enthusiastic expression on his face was so appealing.

'OK,' she agreed in a tone of long-suffering. 'Ten it is.'

'Great!' He straightened up to his feet in one smooth surge of strength, his enthusiasm a balm to Emma's soul.

For the sake of her shattered concentration, it was a good job that the most serious injuries she had to deal with that afternoon were those of cyclist and a skateboarder who'd collided at speed and left several yards of skin on the road.

The whole time she was dealing with removing grit from bare arms and legs and cleaning and dressing their wounds, the two brothers were bickering about whose fault it was, and who had said what about which side they were supposed to cross of the slalom they'd constructed.

'Hey!' Finally Emma was moved to intervene. 'Why don't you do what the professional display teams do when they're setting up stunts?'

'Huh?'

'What?'

Emma nearly smiled at their astonishment that she'd actually said something non-medical, but she knew that at the first sign that she wasn't taking the whole thing as seriously as they were she would lose their attention.

'They practise a series of signals—such as hand movements—which only they know. Then, when they've practised over and over to get it really smooth, they can put on a performance and it looks as if they're reading each other's minds, because no one else knows what the signals mean.'

There were several seconds of blank silence while they gazed at her in awed amazement.

'Wow! Like a secret code,' said one, his surly expression breaking into a gap-toothed grin.

'Fantastic!' said the other, and for the rest of their stay in her care they were busily working together to sort out a plan of campaign for astounding their friends.

'Brilliant!' Barbara Noone praised when Emma finally saw them depart. 'The noise was getting so bad in here that I was just about to come and ask if you needed a hand to negotiate an arms treaty to avert World War Three. I shall try a version of that trick on my nephews next time I get conned into babysitting!'

Although she was tired by the time she reached home, Emma wasn't nearly ready to go to bed. She was almost fizzing with anticipation at the prospect of spending at least part of her day off in Adam's company.

Even the dreaded chores didn't seem so bad when they were accompanied by thoughts of his open pleasure when she'd accepted his invitation, and she laughed aloud at his bossy organisation of her time—almost as if he wanted to spend as much of it with her as possible.

Whatever the reason, it was very flattering to have such a man eager for her company. It was a long time since she had allowed anyone, let alone someone from the male half of the species, close enough to feel that he wanted to go out with her.

Emma gave a little grimace as honesty forced her

to admit that it was probably all her own fault, but she could hardly be blamed for her wariness.

She finally settled under the clean bedcovers in a pristine bedroom in a gleaming flat, with her hair freshly washed and her body sweet and clean in her prettiest cotton nightie.

Her mood was so buoyant that even the intrusion of her mental visitor couldn't dampen the bubbles in her blood, and she welcomed the unusually hesitant connection.

'Come on, then,' she murmured as she allowed her body to relax. 'I'm feeling so…so happy tonight that you can do your worst and it won't get me down…' She took a deep breath and released it, concentrating on filling her mind with positive, welcoming thoughts.

Hope.

The tentative emotion was the last thing she was expecting and she felt her breathing quicken.

Anticipation.

'Me too,' Emma murmured softly. 'Oh, whoever you are, I hope your problems are solving themselves. I know what it's like to travel down that long dark tunnel.'

Perhaps…things can get better.

Emma blinked as, for the first time, the feelings she was picking up almost seemed to take on words instead of being pure emotions.

Perhaps…we can learn to trust…to love….

A prickle of extra awareness made all the hairs on her body stand out, almost like a startled cat's fur.

This was uncanny. Eerie.

This was the first time anything like this had happened and she wasn't sure if she liked it. Was this how Richard had felt when he'd thought that she could read his mind? Because that was just what this mysterious person seemed to be doing.

Either that or the whole episode was some sort of weird rebound so that she was picking up her own emotions. How else could she explain that the feelings she was experiencing from this other person mirrored her own so exactly?

Who else could possibly know her secret desire to trust Adam, her longing to be open with him, to share her thoughts and feelings in the hope that he was sharing the same growing feelings for her?

When the contact was broken Emma was left with a confused jumble of emotions of her own, but the thread which ran strongly through all of them was optimism. For the first time in years she was able to look towards the rest of her life with a feeling of hope.

The optimism was still there when she woke up in the morning, and she was smiling as she dressed in a wellworn pair of jeans in preparation for her outing with Adam. The shirt she chose had seen better days too, but she wasn't totally confident that she'd remember everything she'd learnt years ago and she didn't intend ruining a good shirt in a fall just so that she could impress Adam with her appearance.

The doorbell rang fifteen minutes early but she'd already been waiting impatiently for his arrival for an hour.

'Hi.' Adam's deep voice flowed through her like dark molasses, his eyes gleaming with golden sparks as they travelled over her from head to foot.

'D-do you want to come in a minute while I get my bags from the kitchen?' It felt as if her heart was trying to climb out of her throat.

'Sure.' He shouldered himself away from his comfortable position against the doorpost and prowled past her.

Her eyes were riveted to the lean perfection of his hips and thighs, clad in jeans that clung even more closely than her own.

'Turn left,' she directed him hastily when she managed to drag her gaze away from the tight muscles of his bottom long enough to realise that he was nearly in her bedroom.

'It doesn't look in the least as if it needs a shovel,' he commented as he glanced around.

Every surface gleamed with cleanliness after her frenzied work yesterday evening, but she could hardly tell him that it was his fault she'd put in so much effort.

'It's small, but it's fairly near the hospital and it's affordable.' She shrugged diffidently.

'So, how long before you're ready to go shopping?' He tucked his hands in the front pockets of his jeans as if he didn't quite know what to do with them, his action stretching the faded denim across the blatant evidence of his masculinity.

Emma forced herself to look away and turned to grab the purse and shopping list she'd left ready on the top of her fridge.

'Ready to go,' she said brightly, hoping her lascivious thoughts hadn't shown on her face.

The shopping trip was fun, and she was able to buy several things that she would have had to make a tiring second trip for if she hadn't had the luxury of transport.

'I could get quite used to the idea of having a chauffeur-driven car at my beck and call,' she teased as he locked the various bags and packages in the back of his car.

'Especially if it comes equipped with a driver with long enough arms to get the tins on the top shelves,' he taunted, reminding her of her attempts to reach the last of a special offer, which had rolled right to the back of a display.

'And with the muscles to carry it all back to the car,' she added as he unlocked the passenger door for her. 'Thanks, Adam. I don't remember when shopping was ever this easy—or this much fun.'

'You're welcome,' he murmured close to her ear, and helped her into her seat with innate courtesy.

* * *

It should have taken only a few minutes to unpack the shopping and put it away but Adam insisted on helping, so the whole exercise deteriorated into farce.

Two cups of coffee later they had finally recovered from their laughter enough to set off towards the stables that Adam had discovered, and Emma's stomach filled with a fresh set of butterflies.

'Can I help you?' a young woman called in a cool tone as Emma climbed out of the car.

'I phoned yesterday evening,' Adam began in his distinctive American accent as he straightened up from locking the car.

'Oh, yes,' the woman breathed, her attitude completely different as her eyes travelled over him greedily from head to foot. 'Mr Wolf.'

Emma was torn between offering the woman a bib before she started drooling, or scratching her eyes out, but she bit her tongue and stayed silent.

'You said you had a horse trained for western riding?' he said calmly, as if he hadn't even noticed her reaction to him.

'Yes. I groomed him for you myself—'

'And the other horse has an English saddle?' he broke in briskly.

'Yes—' Her expression was growing distinctly frustrated as he prevented her from saying any more.

'And you were going to look for a large-scale map of the area around that hill.' He pointed to the tree-clad slopes which rose a little way behind the farm-house attached to the stables.

'Yes. It's in the saddle-bag on the western saddle,' she confirmed, with a smile of anticipation.

'Well, if we could mount straight up, we'd like to get on our way,' Adam said politely.

'Oh, but…' Her avid face fell as she glanced up at the clock on the cupola above the entrance to the sta-bles. 'I've got one girl off sick and some tinies coming in for a lesson soon, and the other girl hasn't come back with the other ride.'

'Is that a problem?' Adam enquired, his tone po-liteness itself.

'Well, it means I either have to cancel the tinies class or you'll have to wait until Debbie comes back,' she said, sounding quite flustered.

'Why should that make any difference?'

'Well, it means I'm not free to go with you.' She sounded almost tearful.

'Well,' Adam drawled broadly, 'that's no problem. We'll just take ourselves off for a couple of hours and let you get on with what you have to do.'

'Oh, no. I couldn't do that—' she bleated.

'I thought you said the horses were—what did you call them?—bomb-proof. And I'm sure you said the land surrounding the hill was enclosed by stock-proof fencing.'

'Well…yes.'

'Well, I hardly think we're going to get lost, then, are we? So, if you'll just point our mounts out to us…'

By this time Emma was biting her tongue with a vengeance, and she was glad to leave the whole charade to Adam.

'But they're very valuable horses and I don't even know if you can ride,' the poor girl wailed.

'Well, you aren't likely to find out until you see us on them,' he argued logically, and she sighed heavily and gave in with bad grace.

The animal she led out first was an elegant-looking beast with a body the colour of polished chestnuts and a black mane and tail.

'That one looks like yours,' Adam commented to Emma as it was led towards them. 'Is that about what you were used to?'

'Pretty much,' she confirmed, liking the look of the animal immediately, and taking the time to introduce herself and let him get to know her before she checked the security of saddle and bridle.

'There's a good fella,' she crooned, her voice just above a whisper as she'd learnt from an old Irish horseman, and she smiled to herself as she watched his ears flicker back as he listened.

She was delighted to find that she'd lost none of her old skill as she settled herself in the saddle and prepared herself for a thoroughly enjoyable ride with or without a chaperon.

'Is that the only western saddle you have?' she

heard Adam enquire as a second horse was led out. 'I think it's more of a pony size.'

The horse wasn't a great deal larger than the one that Emma had been given, but he was powerfully muscled, with a characteristic spread of dappled markings, white on the dark coat over his rump.

Emma nearly choked at the incongruous sight of the diminutive saddle on a horse big enough for a powerfully built adult male and waited to see what would happen.

'I'll get an English saddle for you, instead,' the young woman offered.

'Don't bother.' Adam stepped forward and stripped the saddle off with the minimum of fuss. 'I prefer riding without, anyway.' And, after a similar introduction ritual to the one Emma had followed with her mount, he leapt easily onto the back of the powerful animal.

'Oh, my God,' gasped the young woman, clearly impressed with his skill, and a new expression crossed her face. 'I bet you're one of the actors working on that film—or a stunt man,' she guessed again excitedly. 'That's it! You're a stunt man, aren't you? I'm right, aren't I?'

Adam placed one finger against his lips and winked at her before he signalled silently for Emma to follow him.

Emma managed to hold onto her mirth until they were clear of the yard, then burst out laughing.

'I bet you're a stunt man,' she simpered, then reverted to her own voice. 'You're nothing but a big show-off, Adam Wolf.'

'Well, it meant we didn't have to have that empty-headed ninny coming along with us. I'd already told the woman on the phone that we were competent riders and that we were well insured.'

'You speak for yourself,' Emma demurred. 'You might be in practice, but it's years since I last rode, and as for insurance—'

'You ride well,' he broke in. 'You move with the horse as if you were part of him. Who taught you?'

'An old Irishman,' Emma said, a fond smile crossing her face as she remembered the first true friend she'd ever had. 'He'd broken so many bones in his life that he walked like a crab, but on horseback he was a magician.'

As she regained her confidence in herself and her horse she allowed her eyes to stray over the stunning picture that Adam made riding bareback. He was everything old Paddy had been and so much more, the empathy between him and the horse he encircled with powerful thighs evident in the proud carriage of each.

'Your heritage has never been more obvious than it is at the moment,' she murmured with open admiration. 'You look…right.'

There was a sharp question in his eyes when they met hers, but one glance was enough to tell him what she was thinking, and he smiled.

'I feel right too. It's too long since I've been on a

horse and to find an Appaloosa of such quality in an out-of-the-way place…' He shook his head in amazement.

'They are native to America, aren't they?'

'Once they were introduced by the Spanish,' he elaborated. 'Ownership of horses was one of the measures of how well a plains tribe would survive, and the Blackfoot became known as superb horsemen.'

While they were talking they'd reached the track winding its way up the side of the hill towards the summit and entered the cathedral-like hush under the trees.

'I envy people who own land like this,' Emma murmured in a voice suitable for a church.

'To my people, the concept of owning land is alien. Land exists before we do, and will still exist after we go. We can't own it; we are merely caretakers of it for the duration of our time on it.'

Emma was silent for a moment while she thought about the concept. 'That idea makes a lot more sense than the one I've been brought up with, where everyone's intent on grabbing everything they can out of the earth for themselves. Your way means that everyone is bound to take care of the land for the next generation.'

The track was wide enough for the two of them to ride side by side, with a swath of grass up the centre, and for some minutes they rode silently, with bird song and the rhythmic crushing of last autumn's leaves by the horses' hooves the only sounds to break the silence.

'Confident enough for a bit more speed?' Adam said, with a gleam of challenge in his eyes. He looked so at home on the animal he was riding, his body moving easily and naturally with every shift of gait, the powerful muscles of his lean thighs outlined by the worn fabric of his jeans.

'Define speed,' Emma demanded cautiously, dragging her eyes away from his body to concentrate on the knowing expression on his face.

'Oh, just a gentle canter…for a start,' he suggested, and she saw the muscles in his legs tauten as he squeezed with his legs to signal to the horse.

Emma laughed aloud as her own mount responded to her instructions. 'This is great!' She shook her head as the breeze generated by their speed teased tendrils of dark hair from the controlling clip to curl around her face. 'He's got lovely smooth paces.' And she leant forward to urge him on, drawing up level with Adam's mount.

'Faster?' His teeth gleamed whitely in his smiling face.

'OK,' Emma tossed back, accepting the challenge, and their pace increased from the steady three beats of a canter to the faster double beat of a gallop.

The thudding of the horses' hooves on the packed earth echoed back to them off the trunks of the trees and reverberated up through her body like an extra heartbeat, the adrenalin pouring through her as the horses responded to the increasing angle of the hill.

The track widened suddenly and they emerged from the shelter of the trees into the sunshine of the wide, grassy area that sloped up towards the top.

'Whoa, boy, steady.' Adam gentled his mount into a slower pace and Emma did likewise until they were once more walking side by side. 'A couple of minutes to allow them to cool down, then we'll give them a break,' he said as they approached the summit.

'That was fantastic,' Emma panted as she watched Adam jump lightly to the ground. 'I hadn't realised just how much I've missed it.'

'So you're glad you came?' Adam smiled up at her as he looped the reins of his own mount around his arm and reached two hands up to her waist to lift her out of the saddle.

The power of the reaction she felt as soon as his hands touched her was stronger than at any time before in her life, and her secret knowledge of the pleasure he felt as he held her body between his hands redoubled her own awareness of him.

She rested her hands on his shoulders to steady herself, and felt the taut, contained power in his muscles as he lowered her slowly, his breath warming her throat at the open neck of her shirt, then her face as her feet finally reached the ground.

'Fishing for compliments?' she said shakily, her heart racing faster than the echo of the horses' galloping hooves. 'Yes. I'm glad I came.' And she allowed her candid grey eyes to rise from the rapidly beating pulse at the base of his throat to meet the mysterious goldshot darkness of his.

'Emma…?' Adam paused and his hands seemed reluctant to release her. 'Can I ask a favour?' he said hesitantly. 'You can say no if you think it's too much of a liberty…'

'What?' Emma was intrigued.

'Would you let your hair down?'

Emma's breath caught in her throat as she recognised the significance of the slightly hoarse tone in his voice, and her hands rose almost of their own accord to comply with his request.

At the last minute she paused and, keeping her eyes fixed on his, issued a challenge of her own.

'I will if you will,' she murmured huskily, and felt the jolt of awareness hit him.

CHAPTER SIX

'OK,' ADAM murmured, his voice soft and almost dangerous as he raised one hand to pull at the end of the leather thong that bound the dark strands at the base of his skull, his eyes focused on her as intently as lasers.

Midnight-dark silk spilled over his shoulders and he shook his head until it settled to frame the stark purity of his bone structure. As she feasted her eyes on the perfection of him his chin came up, the arrogant gesture throwing his jaw into prominence and accentuating the strength of his cheek-bones and the slightly curved blade of his nose.

'Your turn,' he growled, taking a step towards her. She reached up to release the clasp that tried vainly to control the profusion of her hair, and realized he was already spearing his fingers through the strands as though he couldn't wait to touch them.

'Beautiful,' he breathed. 'It's so full of life. How can you bear to tie it in a knot like that? Hair like this should be free.'

His intensity almost took her breath away and her voice was shaky when she replied. 'I'm sure Nurse Noone would be well impressed if I came on duty with this mess hanging all over the place.' She flicked a dismissive hand at the dark curls spilling over her shoulders and halfway down her back.

'Mess?' He sounded outraged. 'This isn't a mess, it's a glory.' And he buried his face in handfuls of it, smoothing it over the planes of his cheeks as though it were a priceless silken fabric.

'Come on.' He straightened up abruptly and drew in a deep breath as he released her hair. 'Let's settle the horses by some grass and sit down.' He turned, led their two mounts into the shade and tethered them.

Emma was glad that he'd taken charge of her horse, because she was having trouble staying upright, let alone walking, on legs that seemed to have forgotten how to support her.

When he beckoned her to join him at the summit she drew in a deep breath and took the first step, amazed that her knees remembered how to bend, and climbed the last few steps.

Gratefully she sank to the grass and wrapped her arms around her upraised knees, for the first time looking out at the view.

'Oh, Adam, it's fantastic,' she breathed as her eyes took in the vista spread out below them.

The gentle slopes of the valley were a patchwork of soft greens and the bleached gold of ripening fields of grain. The clumps of trees dividing them were in full summer leaf and they created dark patches of shade where sheep and cattle dozed out of the heat of the afternoon.

'How did you find this place?' she questioned, finally dragging her gaze away from the scene in front of her. 'Have you been here before?'

'No, but I looked on a map that showed contour lines to find it. Then, when I saw the ad for the riding school, everything came together.'

'But why were you looking for it in the first place?' Emma was intrigued.

'Wherever I go, I have to find somewhere like this.' He fixed his dark gaze on hers, his words sounding almost like a confession. 'I need the…recharging of batteries that this gives me.' He indicated the scene spread out before them with the wave of one lean hand.

'Have you always done this?'

'Since I was a child. It was something I was taught by my grandfather.'

'Didn't your parents do it, too?'

'I don't remember them,' he said candidly without a trace of self-pity. 'My grandfather took care of me and taught me what I had to do.'

'He's Blackfoot too?'

Adam nodded. 'He's a tribal shaman—a healer.'

'So you're both healers.' Emma smiled her delight. 'He must be so proud of you.'

Adam was silent as a shadow passed over his face, and Emma picked up the echoes of a deep sadness.

'Wasn't he pleased when you wanted to train as a doctor?' she probed gently.

'He said that he had already taught me what my people needed me to know, and that if I went to learn white men's medicine I would end up knowing less as a man than I knew when I was a child.'

'That wasn't fair,' Emma objected. 'There are many things that his traditional skills aren't equipped to deal with. How could he do that to you—make you feel as if you had to make a choice?'

Adam smiled slowly. 'That's how I felt at first. I was angry with him, thinking that he had abandoned me. Then I remembered how he'd taught me to think, to analyse, and I realised that he was making me think about my reasons for making the choice in the first place.'

'Was he disappointed when you chose to become a doctor? Did it cause a rift between you?'

'No. He still believes that I will return to the reservation to take his place before he goes.'

'How old is he?'

'Eighty-six—' Adam smiled '—but he would hate for me to remind him of it.' His smile faded as if he had just remembered something painful.

'What?' Emma prompted softly.

'I went to visit him just before I came over here,' Adam sighed. 'He said the same thing he always does—he's getting too old and when am I going to come back where I belong, where I'm needed the most.' He looked up at her with a deep sadness in his eyes. 'The trouble is, for the first time he sounded as if he meant it, and he seems to have suddenly grown frail.'

'Oh, Adam.' Her heart went out to him and, without thinking, she reached out a hand to rest it on his arm; the jolt of sensation stopped her breathing.

For several seconds they were totally still, her hand resting on the warm strength of his naked forearm, their eyes locked together as though neither of them wanted to break the contact.

'I need—' He broke off, his voice too husky to continue, and closed his eyes, finally releasing her from their spell so that she could remove her hand from the warm seduction of his flesh.

He cleared his throat before he spoke again but Emma was sure that the words were different from those he had been going to say before.

'I need to switch off for a moment. Please, forgive me for being less than hospitable.'

She watched as he settled himself and drew in a deep breath, his chest expanding and stretching the soft knit fabric of his polo shirt over its impressive breadth.

'Is this something that your grandfather taught you too?' Emma murmured softly as she felt herself being enveloped by an aura of peace.

'From when I was very small,' he confirmed, his voice growing distant and low, almost hypnotic. 'I use it as a way of controlling myself when I can't control what's happening around me, a way of bringing myself back into balance…' The words died away on the breeze as she watched the tiny indications of tension leave his face.

Emma, too, made herself comfortable, crossing her legs tailor-fashion and allowing her hands to lie limply on her thighs in her own version of the yoga position, then she closed her eyes and allowed her mind to wander.

Gradually, through the usual kaleidoscopic jumble of images, she began to see a picture in her mind of a towering hill rising out of a tree-clothed plain. As she focused on the mental image she somehow knew that this was a very special place, a place of great power, and that it had a particular significance for Adam.

She suddenly found herself looking at an animal— a large grey wolf whose golden eyes seemed, even in her imagination, to be fixed directly on her. As she watched, mesmerized, she noticed a shadow half-hidden behind the powerful presence of the big grey animal and she fought to see what it was, convinced that it was essential that she should be able to see it.

Eventually the shadow moved to stand beside the big male, and she could see that it too was a wolf but smaller and slighter, with great grey eyes, and she knew with utter certainty that she was the wolf's mate.

* * *

Later that night, after Adam had dropped her at home, Emma was still unable to decide what her vision had meant.

Adam had hardly spoken to her since he'd finally surfaced from their time of silence. He'd almost withdrawn into himself and Emma had known that it had not been the time to tell him what she'd seen or to ask him if he had an explanation.

Even so, she'd felt a strong sense of connection with him since their time together on top of the hill—even stronger than she'd had with the mystery person who had been invading her nights.

As she lay in her bed in the soft darkness she began to wonder if she had been wrong all this time.

Perhaps it was possible to gain enough control over this gift of hers so that she *could* lead a normal life. She now knew two men with whom she felt at ease in a way that she never had before. Adam and her mystery visitor—and somehow over the last few days she had become convinced that the person with whom she'd connected *was* a man—each seemed to seek her company, either mentally or physically.

Maybe there were other people who would accept her for the person she was, without fear or disgust.

Perhaps *Richard* had been the one with the problem. Perhaps it had been *his* failing that he hadn't been able to cope with the fact that she was more sensitive than most to his feelings.

The more she thought about it, the more she realised

that, in all the time he had known her, he had made no effort to find out about her gift but had tried to shut out all knowledge of it so that when an incident had occurred he'd reacted as if Emma had let him down in some way.

She curled up under the softness of her summer-weight duvet and realised that, if Adam hadn't been in such a strange mood this afternoon, she might even have found the courage to tell him about her secret.

Perhaps she was hoping for too much, just because she was so attracted to him, but she honestly believed that when she told him he would understand.

Anyway, a small voice insisted on adding, if she was wrong and Adam did turn out to feel the same way as Richard had, at least he would be returning to America when his three months were over, and she wouldn't have to cope with the trauma of trying to work with someone who despised her.

'Mr Demetriou? This is Nurse Sullivan.' Barbara Noone was trying to attract the attention of the man hunched over in his seat in the waiting area, his hands gripping the back of his skull.

As she continued he straightened gingerly and began to stand up. 'If you will follow her through to—'

'Catch him!' Emma shouted as the man started to go down like a felled tree.

Barbara turned back just in time to grab hold of the

lapel of his jacket, and between that and Emma's grasp of his elbow they managed to slow his fall.

'Trolley, quick!' Barbara directed as she rolled him effortlessly into the recovery position. 'And grab a bit of muscle while you're about it.'

Emma took off, her pace just short of a run as she commandeered a porter and signalled Dave to come with her.

In no time they had the grey-faced patient on the trolley and he was on his way into the emergency room, with Adam Wolf following close behind.

'He staggered into the department under his own steam about fifteen minutes ago, complaining of a terrible headache which had come on very suddenly. He said he felt sick and the light was hurting his eyes and he was a bit confused, but, apart from a slight backache, there were no other obvious symptoms.'

While Nurse Noone had been filling Adam in on the presenting symptoms Emma had been noting down her initial observations of his vital signs, but it wasn't until she came to take his pulse that she received a frightening jolt.

Suddenly, counting his pulse was the least of her worries, and she swung to face Adam just as Barbara left the room.

'Adam,' she said urgently, completely forgetting the proper form of address in the pressure of the situation, 'I...' She paused and swallowed hard in an attempt to control her fear. This was not the way she had wanted it to happen… 'Do…do you think this could be a sub-arachnoid haemorrhage?'

Inside, where she was sensitive to strong emotions, she felt the shock go through him at the same time as she saw the evidence of it cross his face.

'What on earth made you think of that?' The sharp words were accompanied by a rapid examination of the patient, Adam's forehead furrowed in concentration. 'Is there a tray ready for a lumbar puncture?' he directed over his shoulder. 'If there's blood in the cerebrospinal fluid—'

'You can't do that if his intracranial pressure's raised, can you?' Emma turned the essential words into a question, and earned herself another penetrating look and another knife-like stab of hidden suspicion.

'Let's put it this way.' His accent was very clipped. 'If I draw off fluid from his lower spine when the pressure is high in his skull, the imbalance could cause his brain to be sucked through the base of his skull and kill him.

'Now—' he turned to face her, fixing her with a stern gaze '—if you know something—anything—that could affect Mr Demetriou's chances of survival, you'd better tell me.'

Emma clenched her hands tight as she gathered her courage, and her nails bit into her palms as the words came out in jerky spurts.

'He's got a subarachnoid haemorrhage—a berry aneurysm at the base of his brain that's—leaking slightly and it's just about to burst.'

'Thank you.' One hand was already reaching out for the phone to alert Theatre and line up a surgical team.

Emma was still standing beside their patient, her hand holding his wrist.

'I don't know if they can get to it in time,' she murmured, her voice shaky with the strain of what she was doing. 'A small leak can repair itself, but this one is so big…'

Why did it have to be Adam who'd been in the room? With anyone else on the staff she could have found some way of bluffing her way through, trading on her reputation for lucky guesses, but she'd allowed him to get too close…

'How badly is he haemorrhaging?' he said in a low voice as they accompanied the trolley towards the lift.

'It's getting worse by the minute,' she returned almost under her breath as the doors slid closed behind them.

'Right,' Adam muttered, and slid one hand under his skull. As Emma watched in amazement he closed his eyes and grew still, a look of total concentration on his face.

There was a strange sensation in her fingers where they were still grasping Mr Demetriou's wrist and she nearly dropped it in surprise.

'Don't let go.' Adam's voice sounded strangely hollow and guttural. 'Help me...' And he was silent again.

Emma closed her eyes and concentrated on the sensations she was feeling through her hands and in her mind, analysing them carefully until she suddenly realised that Adam was trying to do something impossible—he was trying to control the man's blood pressure by some strange form of will-power, in an attempt to lessen the force on the weakened area of blood vessel.

Oh, she knew *why* he was trying to do it—if he succeeded it would buy their patient a little more time in which the surgical team could operate to save his life. What she didn't know was what gave him the idea that it was even worth trying. What made him think that it was possible for one person to be able to control another's blood pressure by sheer will-power?

Impossible as she knew it to be, it was working. She could tell that the blood loss was slowing rather than increasing...

Deep inside, Emma felt the first stirrings of fear.

Who was Adam Wolf that he had such power? What other frightening powers might he be hiding?

The lift doors slid open and willing hands reached in to pull the trolley straight through for Mr Demetriou to be prepped.

In the general mêlée of people around the patient, Emma slipped silently away and returned to A and E, taking the long way down by the stairs to give herself a little time to think.

Except rational thought seemed to have fled. Nothing made sense any more.

For a moment she wondered if this were all a dream. In a few minutes, would her alarm clock ring so that she could laugh at the outlandish things she had imagined?

She pushed the door open at the foot of the stairwell just as an ambulance drew up outside the entrance to the unit, lights and siren going, and she knew it hadn't been a dream.

She shivered as all the hairs stood up on the back of her neck, and firmly shut a mental door on the events of the last half-hour. Later, when she was safely home in her little flat, she would think about it. Just at the moment, with a young motorcyclist bleeding from multiple injuries, she had far more pressing things to do.

That patient was the start of a hectic time, with a tide of injuries arriving faster than they could be treated, but Emma was grateful, knowing that it meant that there would be no time for Adam to speak to her alone.

She knew he wanted to—the glower on his face when he'd returned to A and E after seeing Mr Demetriou up to Theatre was enough to tell her that he was angry that she'd disappeared without a word. She didn't need any special powers to know that.

In the meantime, there was a patient with a violent allergy to peanuts, a lady with the back of her hand bleeding profusely from an accidental scratch by her dog, a child with a foreign body of some sort stuck up his nose, and a teenager who had developed a septic ear after a less than successful attempt at piercing his own ears.

'We gave her epinephrine to inhale and she's on oxygen via a nasal cannula.' The paramedic was completing his report as he wheeled the patient with the allergy reaction through.

'She apparently brought up most of the contaminated food before we got to her, just after she felt her face flush. She's got a large bore IV running wide open, and we've been picking up some tachycardia on the heart monitor. Her breathing isn't sounding good.'

'Emma?' Dave called across from the opposite room. 'I need you to take over here.'

She glanced in through the open door to see the gory mess on the back of the dog woman's hand and nodded silently.

In a moment the two of them had changed places and Dave was positioning the allergy patient ready for intubation.

'Mrs Larkin? I'm Nurse Sullivan.' She pulled on fresh gloves and checked that everything was ready for her to start work.

'Why did that young man want you to take over?' Her patient was obviously in pain, but there was nothing wrong with her powers of observation.

'If you'd ever seen the way he sews a button on a

shirt, you'd know,' Emma said, with a smile. 'He's a very good technician, but he's the first one to admit that sewing up isn't one of his favourite jobs.'

'So how good are you at needlework?' The answering smile was a little wan, but she was definitely less tense than she'd been when Emma arrived.

'Pretty good,' Emma confirmed. 'Once I get this lot deadened, I can take my time and get it nice and neat.'

'Well, at least I know I haven't got to have a tetanus jab as well this time.' She averted her eyes as Emma prepared to inject along each side of the wound. 'Last time I missed the top step in the garden and gashed my shin. I swear the tetanus shot hurt more than the stitches.'

'I'll need to wait a couple of minutes to make sure that's good and numb, then I'll debride the edge to get a neat join. In the meantime, let's get you cleaned up a bit.'

Emma rinsed the surrounding area with saline before she finally started to draw the two sides of the ragged gash together.

'How on earth did you do this?' she asked, knowing that her patient needed to keep her mind occupied.

'I was playing with the dog and we both went to catch the same ball at the same time. Unfortunately, her tooth caught me right across the back of my hand where the skin's thinnest.'

'Is she a very boisterous dog?'

'Not usually. She's getting quite old and she's a

wonderful guard dog, but so gentle. She was so upset when I shouted, and took herself off to her bed almost as if she was a child being sent to her room. I had to go and tell her I wasn't cross with her before I could come to the hospital.'

The suturing was soon done and her patient finally plucked up the courage to look at Emma's handiwork before she covered it.

'You've made a lovely job of that.' She released a deep sigh of relief and managed a more normal smile. 'The stitches are so small and neat and you've even joined the two halves of my freckle!'

Emma chuckled as she taped a dressing over her work. 'Keep it dry as long as you can so you don't slow the healing down or get an infection in it,' she advised. 'When the local anaesthetic wears off, you'll probably feel better with the hand raised and supported—just until it stops throbbing.'

'Oh, good. That means my husband will have to do the washing-up for a few days!' the woman chuckled, obviously feeling better by the minute. 'I had to come back a week later to have the stitches taken out last time.'

'Well, if you want a week without having to do the washing-up…' Emma raised a teasing eyebrow. 'But they'll probably be ready to come out after five days.'

She sent Mrs Larkin away in a much happier frame of mind, with an invitation to come back at any time if she thought the wound had developed an infection.

'What happened to the child with the foreign body?' Emma asked as she went to find out what was next on the list.

'Removed and gone,' Diane West confirmed. 'It was the butterfly from the back of an earring. Fairly easy to grab once we sat on the little eel to keep it still!'

'And the self-piercing job?'

'Still up for grabs. You can have him if you want him,' she offered.

In the distance she heard the all too familiar sound of Adam's voice and jumped at the chance to be busy when he arrived down this end of the department.

Emma knew that she was being a coward but she needed the chance to get her thoughts in order before she saw him again. She knew that he was going to ask her questions about her gift and she was prepared to answer them—she had already decided that she would tell him before today's traumatic happenings.

The thing she wasn't yet ready to do was find out about the strange powers that Adam seemed to have. She was well accustomed to the idea of being able to pick up other peoples emotions, rather like picking up random stations on a radio. What she had never come across before was someone who could actually direct some energy, some power towards other people.

'Hello. I'm—'

'I'm not going to have to have my ear chopped off,

am I?' the belligerent young man demanded as soon as Emma began speaking.

'Not as far as I know,' she replied blandly as she pulled on a fresh pair of gloves. 'We've got to have a proper look at it to see what the damage is first.'

She beckoned for him to sit on the chair beside the sink and handed him a stainless steel kidney bowl.

'Hold this on your shoulder so it's right up against your neck,' she directed, then began to explore. 'How long ago did you do this?'

'About ten days— Ow!' He turned a little to glare up at her. 'You're enjoying this, aren't you?' he accused.

'Of course we do. That's why we become nurses— so we can hurt people.' Emma concentrated on what she was doing as she said the ridiculous words in a deceptively calm voice. She had the dubious pleasure of watching his neck turn a dull red, the colour travelling right up under his semi-shaven hairstyle.

'How many holes did you put in here?' she demanded as she carefully probed the swollen lobe of his ear.

'Six.'

'What sort of earrings did you put in? Gold sleepers?'

'Nah. Studs.'

'Ah!' Emma knew what she was feeling now. 'When did you take the studs out?'

'This morning. It was all swollen and I'd lost one of them...'

'It's not lost,' Emma announced as she straightened up. 'The flesh of your earlobe didn't heal up properly around the hole you made and an infection started. When it started swelling, there wasn't enough space between the stud and the butterfly on the back and they've burst into the lobe.'

'Oh, gross!' The young tough began to look distinctly green. 'Does that mean it's stuck in there?'

'No. It'll have to come out or the infection won't be able to clear.'

'How will you get it out?' There was no sign of the belligerence now. He had become just another apprehensive patient.

'I'll get the doctor, but I think he'll give you an injection to deaden the ear, then go fishing for it.'

'Will you be here?' He refused to look at her, but Emma was careful not to smile at the change in his attitude.

'Wouldn't miss it for the world,' she assured him breezily. 'You know how we nurses are into other people's pain.'

His head shot round towards her, his eyes wide with shock, and she threw him a grin and a wink as she went to organise the next stage.

Her luck was holding because, when she went looking for him, Adam was fully occupied in one of the emergency rooms and it was the senior house officer who came to retrieve the embedded jewellery.

Adam was still busy when she went off duty, and she arrived home with a sense of relief, locked her door behind her and collapsed in a heap in the corner of her slightly lumpy sofa.

She kicked her shoes off, and took the clasp out of her hair to relieve the tension headache which had been building ever since she'd realised what was wrong with Mr Demetriou.

She'd been glad to hear that he'd survived the process of repairing the damaged blood vessel at the base of his brain. Now his family just had to wait and see how much residual damage he would be left with.

She must have dozed off in spite of her less than comfortable position, because the evening shadows were filling the room when she woke up with a jump, all the hairs going up on the back of her neck.

'Who's there?' she whispered, her eyes darting about apprehensively. Was someone in her flat? How had they got in? She was sure that she'd locked the door when she'd returned from her shift.

CHAPTER SEVEN

ARE you there?

The sensation of her mystery visitor arriving in her mind unannounced had become familiar now, and she found herself relaxing as relief flowed over her.

'Yes, I'm here,' she murmured aloud into the quiet of her room, glad that it was only *his* presence she had felt and not some intruder's.

She let her head drop back against the high back of the sofa with a snort of disbelief. 'It's a good job no one can hear me. They'd think I was one sandwich short of a picnic to be sitting in the dark talking to myself.'

Even so, she stayed where she was and waited. After her fierce determination that she wasn't going to allow any communication with this intrusive stranger, she was surprised how welcome the contact had become.

She didn't know whether the knowledge that she was listening had helped him to feel less alone with his problem, but she did know that in a strange way the experience of making contact willingly had changed her.

Somehow, since she had given in to the inevitable

and accepted his intrusion into her life, she had felt more at peace with herself and who she was...until today...

I need to speak to you. I'm so confused. I need some answers.

'Don't we all?' Emma muttered as she remembered again her growing fear at the sudden realisation that Adam wasn't what she had thought.

Oh, she'd known that he wasn't a man who let his emotions show. He spoke very little about himself during his hours on duty, working unstintingly to make his brief stay at such a centre of excellence for multiple trauma a learning experience in both directions.

In spite of all the offers he must have had from the various members of staff since he'd arrived at St Lawrence's, he had, she'd noticed, kept mostly to himself in his off-duty hours. When he had asked her to spend the day with him, her foolish vanity had made her believe that for some reason he had been attracted to her. She had wanted to believe that they were developing some sort of relationship—a friendship.

Now she realised that she hadn't known him at all. How could she, with her sensitivity to other people, have missed such a thing?

She couldn't forget the fear that had slid insidiously inside her when she had realised what he was trying to do for Mr Demetriou, and then the utter disbelief when he'd seemed to achieve it. Surely she must have imagined it? It just wasn't possible for one person to

use his will-power to affect another in that way—
was it?

And, if it was, what sort of person was he that he
had such power…?

*I'm afraid that I might be making a mistake. I might
already have made a serious mistake. I need to try to
sort it out, but I don't know if—*

The sharp knock at her door broke her concentration
and the connection was lost, leaving Emma frustrated.
It was the clearest communication she had ever had
with another person, almost as if she could hear him
speaking directly into her head. Every word had been
as clear as if he had been talking to her face to face,
but, as well as that, she'd been picking up the emotions behind the words…

The knock came again and she glanced across at the
clock on top of her television, peering through the
gloom to decipher the hands.

It wasn't terribly late, not even ten, but she didn't
usually have people calling at this time of night and
her sense of self-preservation kicked in.

In stockinged feet she padded silently over to the
spyhole in the door, to see who it was.

Adam. Her lips shaped his name soundlessly, and
her heart leapt up into her mouth then sank like a
stone. She wasn't ready for this confrontation and she
certainly didn't feel comfortable that it should take
place in her flat, where she would be totally alone
with him…

'Emma.' His deep voice reached her through the door, his tone as soft as though he knew that she was only inches away, with her hungry gaze riveted to the stark planes of his face.

She felt a swift stab of sympathy when she saw how tired and drawn he looked in the dim light of the hallway. For the first time since she'd met him, his broad shoulders were slumped with weariness.

'We need to talk,' he murmured, his dark eyes focusing on the spyhole as though he could see her watching him. 'Please…?'

There was no way she could refuse him when she knew how much it was costing him to plead. He was far too proud a man for that to be easy. As if it was acting without her volition, her hand lifted to release the safety chain and turn the catch.

Wordlessly they gazed at each other for several long seconds before she stepped back to allow him to enter. As Adam went on into the lounge Emma closed and secured the door, the subdued rattle of the chain sending a little shiver up her spine, to tighten the skin on the back of her neck.

She was alone with Adam Wolf, locked in her flat with a man who frightened her—

Stop it! She gave herself a mental shake. That was sheer stupidity. She knew beyond a doubt that he would never physically harm her.

Her silent steps took her into the tiny lounge area, to find it still in darkness. Adam hadn't switched on the light but was standing at the window, looking out at the night.

'Would you rather I left?'

The deep voice travelled through the silence to wrap itself around her and, in spite of her fears, she felt herself relax. This was Adam, the doctor she worked with, who spent his days helping to save lives. Inside her, where she was ruled by instinct, she knew that he was a kind and caring man.

'No,' she sighed. 'Stay.' There was nothing to be gained by delaying this meeting.

'Would you like something to drink?' She reached out a hand to switch on a light.

'Don't.'

The single word held her hand poised by the switch and her head swung towards him to see that he was still facing out into the darkness.

'It might be more comfortable for both of us if we were allowed a semblance of privacy. We have too many things to say that might not stand the glare of light…'

Emma nodded even though he wasn't watching, and went to sit down in the small fireside chair on the other side of the room, tucking her stockinged feet underneath her and wrapping her arms around her as if she was chilled.

'May I sit?' The request underlined his effortless courtesy in spite of the tension filling the room, and she smiled fleetingly as she held one hand out towards the sofa in invitation.

There was a longer silence once he had subsided into her own favourite corner and stretched his long legs out. She heard the squeak of leather as he crossed his ankles the way he always did in the staffroom, and she visualised the way he would then link his fingers together and rest his hands over the buckle of his belt.

'Are you still frightened?'

Emma blinked. It was the first time she had known anyone to be able to see behind her careful façade—but then she should have expected it. Adam Wolf was unlike any man she'd ever known.

'Not frightened, exactly…' She didn't know quite how to describe her emotions.

'If you weren't frightened, why did you run away from me?'

'I didn't—!'

'And why did you spend the rest of the day avoiding me?' He ignored her attempted denial.

Emma was silent for a moment. He was right, she admitted silently. She *had* been running away and she *had* gone to great lengths to make sure that she hadn't had to work with him for the rest of her shift. And what had it gained her? A few hours' grace, which had done her no good at all because she hadn't had a coherent thought since it had happened.

'I wasn't ready to talk to you,' she said honestly,

her chin tilting up in a determined way. 'I needed time to think.'

'And are you ready now?' There was a roughness to his voice, a touch of gravel which revealed his own tension.

'No.' She shook her head. 'I haven't been *able* to think. It's as if my brain has blown a fuse or something and it can't make sense of what it saw...'

'Well, forget your brain. What do your instincts tell you?'

'To run,' she retorted, and he gave a soft huff of appreciative laughter.

'Point taken,' he conceded, and drew in a deep breath before letting it out in a sigh.

Silence fell between them again, but this time the tension was less.

'I feel guilty.' His words finally broke the stillness. 'I should have been able to warn you what I was going to try, but there wasn't time.'

'I probably wouldn't have believed you anyway,' Emma countered bluntly. 'If you'd said you were going to try to control Mr Demetriou's bleeding by mentally lowering his blood pressure—'

'I knew it!' His voice was quietly jubilant in the darkness. 'I knew you could sense what I was doing— I could feel it.'

'I had my fingers over his pulse.' In an automatic reflex, Emma began to cover up the evidence of her ability, her pulse starting to race as it always did when there was danger of discovery and exposure. She couldn't bear to go through that again. 'I could feel—'

'No!' he growled. 'No evasions, no lies—not now. Not between the two of us. This is too important to play games.'

Emma subsided, the slender fingers knotted together on her lap the only outward evidence of her tension.

Finally, 'No, you're right,' she admitted. 'Denial at this late stage is a little pointless.'

'How long have you known?' he questioned.

'Known?'

'About my gift?' His tone was slightly impatient.

'I didn't. Not until Mr Demetriou…' She was surprised that he had to ask. 'That's why it was such a shock.'

'But…you've been picking up my thoughts for some time now—'

'No—' Emma hurried to correct him, the way she always had with Richard '—not your thoughts, just an impression of your feelings. I…it's happened ever since I can remember, especially when people touch me…' Her voice died away with the enormity of her admission.

The last time she'd spoken of it had been to the man she'd hoped to marry, and in the end it had caused him to turn away from her.

She was glad to be sitting in the dark now, as the shame she'd been made to feel all her life filled her face with heat. At least she didn't have to watch the expression on his face change as he realised what a freak she was.

'Which side of your family did the gift come from?'

She could hardly believe how matter-of-fact he sounded, as if he heard such things every day of his life.

'My…my mother's,' she stammered while she fought for mental balance. 'And it's hardly a gift,' she argued. 'In my family it's been more like a curse. It's ruined so many lives…' She was unable to prevent the bitterness colouring her tone.

'I get mine from both sides,' he said quietly.

'You…?' His words robbed her of breath.

'For generations my mother's family were shamans for one branch of the Blackfoot and my father's family held a similar position in a parallel branch.'

'And you inherited their skills?'

'I wish it had been that easy,' he laughed. 'I inherited their gift but I had to *learn* the skills.'

'What do you mean?' She was intrigued.

'I would rather have been taking part in the more active side of life, with my peers, but my grandfather was a hard taskmaster and insisted I must learn how to recognise the many medicinal plants and how to prepare them. Then there was the spiritual side of being a shaman…' He was obviously lost in memories.

'So the Blackfoot don't shun people who have our sort of inheritance?' The very idea was like a revelation. And how strange it felt to have someone to identify with. Apart from her mother, who had tried to obliterate all trace of the 'taint', she had never met anyone like herself before.

'Far from it,' he confirmed. 'Shamans have a very important place within the structure of the tribe, both medical and spiritual.'

'Was it very difficult for you to reconcile what you already knew with what you learnt at medical school?'

'It wasn't as different as you might think. Oh, I had to do a great deal of book learning, where the shaman's teaching is mostly a verbal tradition, but, as far as dealing with patients is concerned, there is very little difference. One thing I recognised very early on is that the use of placebos in medicine seems to be universal, no matter what tradition you follow.'

The silence that spread then was a thoughtful one as Emma fought to alter all her preconceptions.

'When did you suspect that I had the gift too?'

'The first time you tried to cover it up.' She heard humour in his voice. 'You might think you're good at keeping a poker-face, but I knew immediately that you were hiding something.'

'Why didn't you say anything?'

'In case I was wrong. I *do* know about the sort of horrified reaction you've always met, but I was lucky enough not to come up against it until later in life, when I was already certain of the value of what I had.'

Emma envied him that certainty.

'Why did your grandfather teach you? Why not your parents?'

'When they were killed in a fire, trying to help others to safety, Grandfather took on the job of raising me. I was too young to know the difference.'

'Does your grandfather think you'd make a good shaman?'

'He complains that studying Western medicine has ruined all the work he put into teaching me the Blackfoot ways!' There was a wealth of love and respect in his words, but Emma wondered about the reality.

'Does he mean it? Does he resent the choice you made?'

'No, he's far too wise for that. He realises that we have become westernised over the years since the white men came and we are now prey to the white men's diseases.'

'In what way?'

'When we were dependent on hunting and gathering to supply our needs we had to stay fit and healthy or we wouldn't survive the hunt or the long, hard winters. Then we were confined to reservations, with insufficient food and nothing to do, and our numbers fell as we starved to death each winter because we were not allowed to leave the reservation to hunt.

'Now we still have many people living from hand to mouth in poverty, subsisting on welfare cheques, but we also have those who have become very wealthy and are suffering from obesity and heart disease, lung cancer, alcohol addiction, diabetes... The list goes on.'

'And, because these illnesses are so new in Blackfoot society, the shamans are still trying to deal with the new plagues?'

'Exactly. And in most cases it's beyond them, but they can't admit it. In times gone by, if a shaman had several patients in a row die, he was deemed to have lost his powers and he would be killed.'

Emma gave a startled laugh. 'It's a good job we don't apply the same criterion in Western medicine or some branches would soon be running out of practitioners!'

There was a stillness between them as though they had each managed to come to terms with what the other represented, and Emma was exploring the strange delight of knowing someone with whom she could speak about the problems and joys of something that she had only ever thought of as a curse before.

With this link between herself and Adam, perhaps he would feel moved to keep in touch with her even after he returned to America at the end of his three months.

'I'm thinking of extending my stay in England,' he murmured, as if he had been following the same train of thought. 'I'm due some holiday time and I was thinking of spending it exploring this area.'

'It's a beautiful part of the country,' Emma confirmed smoothly, not wanting to betray the leap of her heart at the thought that he might want to stay close to her for a while longer.

The cautious side of her nature was beginning to ring alarm bells. She had already realised that she was drawn to Adam—far more strongly than she had been to any other man. Even Richard hadn't been able to affect her as intensely as Adam did just by walking into a room.

The revelation that they had something so basic…so powerful…in common made the bond between them almost unique. She was becoming far too close to Adam Wolf—close enough that it would be like an amputation when he finally left.

'If I do stay on longer, would you be willing to spend your off-duty time with me?' His rich voice was so tempting, flowing around her in the still of her room.

She closed her eyes to concentrate her thoughts. Even the shadowy outline of Adam's broad shoulders and proud head were enough to distract her from the decision that she had to make.

'I don't know if that would be a good idea,' she said softly, an ache already beginning to gather around her heart at the thought of the time with him that she would be missing.

'Why not?' he challenged. 'I would have thought it would be an ideal opportunity for you to learn a little more about your gift from someone who could teach you how to develop it, how to turn it to good advantage after all this time of looking on it as a curse. You could turn it into a powerful tool to help you in your work.'

Perhaps, a stray thought suddenly popped into her head, she might even learn how to refine her skill so that she could communicate with her midnight stranger. At least that contact might go some way towards the loss of Adam's presence later on. Perhaps, if she became more skilled, she might even find other people with whom she could 'speak'.

'Can we be friends?' she suggested tentatively. 'I'd rather not spend time outside work with you if it can't be as friends.'

He was silent so long that she began to wonder if he was ever going to answer.

'Are you afraid that I'll try to force my attentions on you?' His voice was low and dangerous, as though she had accused him of something; as though she had insulted his honour.

'No!' The word was vehement. 'Never that.'

'Then why the stipulation?' he demanded.

'Because I'm afraid of getting hurt,' she said flatly, realising that only the truth would convince him. 'If we spend our off-duty hours together we can't help getting to know each other and growing close, especially as we're both basically lonely people.'

He made a sound of agreement.

'If we become more than friends in the time before you go, the loneliness will be worse than if I'd never met you. At least if we remain friends there will be something for me to remember with pleasure.'

'You don't think it would be a pleasure to become lovers?' His voice was like pure velvet, stroking over her skin until every nerve was quivering.

She was unaccustomed to sexual banter, and her embarrassment at his sophisticated taunt loosened her control on her tongue so that she abandoned diplomacy for bluntness.

'I've no idea, and I've no intention of finding out with someone who's going back to the other side of the world in a few weeks.'

She heard his sharply drawn breath but to her intense relief he didn't retaliate.

'If that's the way you want it,' he agreed quietly just as she was beginning to think that he would refuse. 'If you'll be happier that way, I promise that we'll just be friends while I'm over here.'

He left soon after that, refusing Emma's offer of coffee. The light in the hallway was too dim to show her any more than his usual self-contained expression, his eyes deeply shadowed and inscrutable as he made his goodbyes.

Emma delayed closing her door, surreptitiously watching his long legs eating up the distance as he walked away from her, until he disappeared round the corner.

'Adolescent nonsense,' she muttered disgustedly as

she slid the chain into position and wandered through to her bedroom.

Having gained his agreement so easily, Emma couldn't understand why she felt so disappointed. Surely she should have been pleased that he had agreed to her wishes? Or, in her heart of hearts, had she secretly wished that he would refuse, that he would say he found her too desirable to contemplate a platonic relationship with her?

'Chance would be a fine thing.' She quoted her mother's favourite maxim as she got ready for bed. 'A man like that, as well qualified as he is and looking as fantastic as he does, could take his pick of willing women.'

Her cheeks blazed as she suddenly realised how presumptuous she must have sounded when she'd told him that she wouldn't have an intimate relationship with him.

'He probably hadn't even thought of asking me,' she moaned in an agony of embarrassment. 'Trust me to make an idiot of myself.' And she dived under the bedclothes to hide her face.

They were both due on duty tomorrow so she would soon know whether he still wanted to have anything to do with her. No wonder he hadn't been able to wait to leave this evening.

In spite of the way the evening had ended she couldn't regret the fact that he'd decided to confront her. They'd spoken about things that needed to be said and she'd learnt so much about him.

She fell asleep trying to imagine what he'd looked like as a child, his solemn little face breaking into that heart-stopping smile and his eyes gleaming with humour…

When her thoughts became dreams she didn't know, but she woke just before her alarm was due to go off, with her heart beating heavily.

'Adam…' she murmured, her voice husky with arousal, and slid one hand out across the wildly rumpled bedclothes…but there was no one there.

'Oh!' Realisation was slow, but eventually she woke up enough to realise that she'd been having the most erotic dream of her life.

She tilted her head back against the pillow to gaze at the ceiling while she willed her pulse to slow and her breathing to steady. It would take longer for the other evidence of her body's aroused state to disappear and she doubted if a cold shower would be the answer.

'How am I ever going to be able to look him in the face?' she groaned. 'Yesterday evening I almost accused him of lusting after my body, and I spent all last night lusting after his!' She shivered sensually as she remembered how she had run her hands over the smooth, warm copper of his naked shoulders and down the lean length of his back, until she'd cupped the tight curves of his buttocks in her hands.

'Stop it!' she wailed, and kicked the duvet onto the

floor to scramble to her feet. The fine cotton of her nightdress untangled itself from around her body and slid down to cover her nakedness, the brush of the delicate fabric over her sensitised skin enough to make her moan with dismay.

Emma arrived at the start of her shift just as an old Mini came hurtling up the slope towards the main entrance.

'Nurse, help!' a voice shouted before the door was properly open. 'The baby fell in the bath—she's not breathing!'

Emma met the distraught mother halfway, grabbed the limp child and set off at a run towards the nearest emergency room.

'Call Dr Wolf,' she threw over her shoulder at the reception desk. 'Near drowning.' And she disappeared through the doors.

Before they had time to swing shut behind her they were thrust open again as a young nurse followed her through.

'I need to intubate,' Emma said between administering mouth-to-mouth resuscitation. 'The tube needs to be the same size as the child's little finger.' She concentrated on maintaining the rhythm of the resuscitation procedure while she listened to the sounds of equipment being gathered.

'Ready, Nurse.' A gloved hand held the laryngoscope in her field of vision and Emma made short work of sliding the blade over the tongue and between the vocal cords.

'Hundred per cent oxygen,' Emma directed. 'Then we need to start an IV and get a nasogastric tube down to decompress the stomach.'

She was just suiting her actions to her words when the doors swung open behind her.

'How far have you got?' Adam's voice was approaching at speed.

'Intubated and receiving hundred per cent oxygen on assisted ventilation, and that's the IV in and running.' She held her hand out and the young nurse handed Emma the last of the prepared strips to tape the IV tube in position.

'Good,' Adam muttered as he administered the appropriate dose of sodium bicarbonate. 'Get that blood sample checked for haemoglobin, blood gases, electrolytes and urea. What's her temperature?'

'Thirty-six, rectal. Blood pressure eight-five over sixty,' she recited as she deftly threaded a nasogastric tube into position. 'Ready to empty the stomach.' She straightened up from positioning the bowl.

The atmosphere in the room grew tense as the seconds ticked remorselessly away and their little charge hardly seemed to be responding to their efforts.

Emma hated this side of her work, having to face the possibility that they couldn't save all of their patients all of the time, especially when they were little children.

Suddenly, among the frantic bleeps and mutters there was a choked cry of distress and the little limbs jerked in protest.

'All right!' Adam drawled the Americanism in a voice full of relief. 'Welcome back to the world, little angel.' And the tender way he smoothed the straggle of blonde hair away from the child's pale, sweaty forehead made Emma's eyes fill with tears.

'Who gets to give the parents the good news?' His tone was definitely upbeat. 'Would you like to send them in here, then arrange for her to be admitted overnight for observation?'

Emma nodded, grateful for the few seconds to get a grip on herself. If she wasn't careful, she'd arrive in the little waiting room with tears running down her face and the poor parents would believe that the worst had happened.

The feeling of euphoria after little Sophie's resuscitation had spread right through the department like a happy ray of sunshine, so the sudden warning of impending multiple casualties was like a slap in the face.

'There's been some sort of gang warfare out on one of the housing estates. Probably a dispute about territory or something. About fifteen casualties with various injuries, mostly from knives and bats,' the message came through. 'Probable involvement with drugs.'

'Right, people,' Adam warned, 'I don't know what

your usual system is here, but back home we assume that everyone involved with the drugs scene is HIV positive and take precautions accordingly. They are our patients and we'll do our best for them while they're in our care, but it's not worth risking our own lives for them.'

It was a sobering message, but, even more, it was a sign of the times they were living in, Emma thought as she checked supplies of gloves, masks and gowns.

The first ambulance full of injuries was accompanied by a couple of burly policemen.

'If you let us know where to go so we won't be in your way,' the more senior one said to Adam, 'we'll just make sure that they behave themselves while they're here. Some of them will be taken away to be charged as soon as you've finished patching them up, but we don't want to risk them starting in on each other again while they're here.'

'Fine by me.' Adam reached out one hand towards the first of his charges. 'If you can identify the different gangs, perhaps you can line them up on opposite sides of the reception area.' He grimaced his sympathy at the policemen's task then beckoned Emma to follow.

The next two hours were filled with a stream of injuries bearing witness to the groups' fondness for knives and baseball bats.

'Do you think they used them because they wanted me to feel at home?' Adam quipped as he sent yet another set of ribs up for X-ray, and sat down with a fresh tray to begin suturing a vicious knife-slash across a teenage bicep. 'So far, we've had one fractured skull, two broken arms, one broken leg, assorted broken ribs, and more sutures than I like to think about.'

'Just like home, in fact,' Emma joked.

'Yeah, but I wasn't expecting to find it here,' he objected. 'I thought it would be what I call *real* accidents, not so many deliberately inflicted injuries.'

He finished the last of a neat row of stitches just as Dave Maddox stuck his head round the door.

'Doctor? Can you come and look at the one in Emergency Two? I think we've got some nerve damage where the injury crosses the palm.'

'If Nurse Sullivan will finish putting a dressing on my customer?' He raised a dark eyebrow.

'Fine,' Emma nodded and was reaching for the appropriate package before the door had swung closed behind them. 'Right, now, Shane.' With a professional smile, she turned to the shifty-looking young man and reached out for the package of dressings. 'Let's get this lot covered up and then you—' The words ended on a gasp when his uninjured arm came up to brandish a wicked-looking blade.

'Right, bitch,' he spat as he grabbed her outstretched hand and twisted it painfully, positioning the point of the knife at the side of her neck. He slid carefully off the side of the trolley until his feet met the floor, and gave an extra twist on her wrist to bring her hand right up between her shoulderblades.

'You're going to get me some stuff before I get out of here,' he hissed menacingly. 'The bloody pigs took everything I'd got except this.' He moved the cold steel against her skin and she felt the sharp bite of the tip as he pressed it harder against her.

CHAPTER EIGHT

'NOT a word,' the youth warned as Emma went to open her mouth, his voice too low to draw attention. 'You make one sound and I'll cut you. Understand? I ain't going to go cold turkey.'

Emma knew that he was referring to the traumatic effects of a sudden withdrawal of an addict's drugs, and understood that just the thought of going through it was enough to make him desperate.

She swallowed and felt the knife press a little harder, knowing that, whether he realised it or not, her assailant had positioned his weapon right over the carotid artery.

One false move and it wouldn't take many minutes before she died.

Everything inside her made her want to let out a blood-curdling scream, but logic told her that the young addict was already jumpy enough. If she gave in to her instincts, it would probably be the last thing she ever did.

Adam!

She closed her eyes and concentrated on her favourite mental image of him—his face filled with laughter as they'd galloped up the hill towards a meadow full of sunshine.

Why had she been such a coward? If she'd told him that day how she'd felt about him…

'Saying your prayers, are you?' the young thug sneered as he gave her arm another yank upwards. 'Well, we haven't got time for that. Just get me some stuff and be quick about it.'

Emma felt sick as she picked up a mental image of the damage the young man had already done to himself with his drug abuse, her dread becoming outright terror when she realised that his craving meant that he was no longer rational.

Help me! Somebody…

She started to put her free hand down towards her pocket where the drugs key rested on the end of its chain. She didn't dare speak for fear that the edge of the blade might slice through those few millimetres which meant the difference between life and death, but, if she showed her willingness, perhaps she could persuade him… But before she reached her goal he stopped her, mistaking her intention.

'Hey, bitch!' he snarled close to her ear, giving an extra jerk on her captive wrist. 'What're you trying to pull? Ain't no one can do anything for you now—not till you get what I want.'

Drugs. He wants drugs.

She nearly laughed at the futility of it all. She knew that she couldn't speak to anyone, couldn't even open her mouth to call for help, and yet here she was trying to send a message by telepathy to someone she'd never met except in her head.

'Shane…?' She had to try to reason with him, had to try to calm him down enough to—

'Shut up, bitch.' He began to drag her over towards the row of cupboards, his hand tightening on the knife so that it angled even closer to that vital artery. 'Is this where you keep the stuff?'

If only the local anaesthetic would start wearing off, Emma yearned. He wouldn't be able to hold the knife so easily then, and she might be able to get away…

Hold on. I'm coming.

Emma stiffened with disbelief.

Somehow, for the first time in her life, she had actually managed to make contact. Her mysterious midnight stranger had heard her terrified messages and had found her. He was coming to help…

He's got a knife. Be careful. She closed her eyes tight as she concentrated on visualising the scene in the treatment room. If she had been able to 'speak' to him, perhaps she could also 'show' him what he was walking into.

'Nurse? Have you finished with that dressing?' Adam's deep, accented voice preceded him into the festering silence of the room as he pushed open the doors with his shoulder.

Adam! No!

Emma's heart was in her mouth as she stood frozen with horror. As she watched, mesmerised, Adam walked in without so much as lifting his eyes from the clipboard in his hand, and walked briskly across the room with all the assurance of a man at home in his own front room.

Get ready...

The voice of the midnight stranger spoke to her in the silence, electrifying every cell with the impossibility of his presence, but in the life-or-death situation unfolding in front of her there was no time for her brain to struggle with its confusion.

Her captor's grasp had tightened ominously as the intruder burst in on them, the knife pressing dangerously against the soft skin of her vulnerable throat. Emma felt the confusion pour through him as the big, white-coated man seemed totally to ignore his presence in the room, and he relaxed his grip slightly.

'Here. Catch!' Without warning, without even seeming to look in their direction, Adam flipped the clipboard towards the grotesque tableau formed by the motionless bodies of the two of them.

Automatically, they both reacted as it sailed towards the unprotected wound on Shane's injured arm— Emma trying to catch it, and her captor ducking out of its way.

Adam's long arm shot out to grab Emma's reaching hand just as her captor's grip loosened on her wrist, and she was dragged out of his grasp and swung across the room and out of danger.

'Bastard!' the young punk snarled, and lashed out at Adam with the knife.

He only had time for one sweeping motion before Adam's longer reach enabled him to deal a swift back-hander to the boy's chin, which snapped his unkempt head back against the bank of cupboard doors.

From her position on the other side of the room Emma watched while, as if in slow motion, Shane slid down into a crumpled heap on the floor.

As he slumped into semi-consciousness he lost his grip on the knife, which landed with a metallic clatter at his feet, gleaming intermittently under the bright lights as it spun lazily to a halt.

'Are you all right?' Adam kicked the knife away and knelt down to check the young addict's vital signs just before the two policemen burst on the scene, his swift glance up at Emma's white face telling her that his concern was for her.

'Y-yes. I'm fine.' Her teeth were beginning to chatter as reaction set in. 'What about you? Did the knife touch you?'

Adam straightened up, with a slight grimace, to face the two uniformed men.

'The knife is over on the other side of the room. Neither of us has touched it. He had Nurse Sullivan here held at knife-point, demanding that she get drugs for him.' He glanced across at her briefly, his eyes glittering with anger. 'She has the mark of the blade on her neck.'

Directed by their gaze, Emma's fingers came up wonderingly to touch the sting at the side of her neck, and they came away sticky from the trickle of blood she encountered.

A mumble from the bundle of humanity on the floor drew their eyes away from her and she observed numbly as they hauled him to his feet, pausing for the few seconds it took to secure a dressing over his recently stitched wound before they unceremoniously frog-marched him out of the room.

'We'll need a statement from you, miss,' one of the policemen tossed over his shoulder as he let the doors slap shut behind them.

'Tomorrow will do,' Adam growled after them. 'She's in no state to do it today.' And he finally turned to walk towards her.

Unable to help herself, she allowed her eyes to travel over him, from the stern austerity of his drawn face to the broad shoulders and clenched fists and...

'Adam! You're bleeding!' She reached a hand out to his side where bright red was beginning to stain the white of his shirt. 'He cut you!'

'It's nothing,' he said dismissively as he reached out one hand to turn her chin gently to allow him to examine her own injury.

As soon as the contact was made she was instantly overwhelmed by a tidal wave of emotions, as his tender concern for her fought with blazing anger that she'd been hurt.

'Are you all right?' he repeated, his fingers tracing the curve of her jaw.

Were her teeth still chattering or was it his fingers that trembled against her? She couldn't tell. She didn't know anything any more…

'Oh, Adam—'

'Excuse me,' an apologetic voice broke in as the door opened again to reveal the younger policeman. 'I've come for the knife.' He held up a self-sealing plastic bag.

Emma took the opportunity to step back, breaking the contact with Adam's gentle touch without losing the incredible sense of connection.

'I…I'll send someone in to clean up in here,' she stammered, backing towards the door, not daring to meet his eyes for fear of what she might see, what she might learn.

'As soon as you've got that organised, come back in here and I'll check you over. You'll need a dressing on that knife wound.' There was a lingering huskiness in his voice which called to her, but she had to resist. She needed to understand what had happened between the two of them today before she could allow him to come any closer.

'As soon as you've had your ribs attended to,' she countered with a touch of bravado. 'My scratch might be in a more dangerous place but I'm not bleeding like a stuck pig.' And she made her escape.

She grabbed Dave between patients and got him to

clean her neck of dried blood and apply an unobtrusive dressing.

'Looks as if you had a rather violent run-in with Count Dracula,' he commented, with an evil leer, then sobered. 'I feel terribly guilty, Em,' he confessed in a low voice. 'If I hadn't called Dr Wolf out to check on my patient it would never have happened.'

'There was no way you could have known what was going to happen. None of us did,' Emma tried to re-assure him. 'He was very lippy and belligerent while we were sorting him out, but no one had any idea he'd flip like that—otherwise the police wouldn't have left him alone with us. They'd have been supervising him every step of the way.' She pulled a wry face. 'It was just unfortunate he decided I looked like a soft touch.'

By the time she had been cleaned up and patched up, Dave was looking more cheerful and Emma's shakiness had subsided, her recovery helped along by a large mug of hot, sweet tea.

When she reported back for the last hour of her shift, Barbara Noone commended her devotion to duty but insisted that she needed to go home and have a good night's sleep to help her get over the trauma of the day's events.

'Tomorrow morning will be quite soon enough to get back in the swing of things,' she said firmly. 'I can't have my staff neglecting their own health.' And she sent Emma off to collect her belongings.

As Emma slid her arms into a light cardigan she

kept in her locker for emergencies, she could hear
Adam's voice at the other end of the corridor and wondered if he had stopped to have his own wound attended to.

Every instinct she possessed made her want to be
the one to take care of him herself, but she knew that
she wasn't in a fit state yet to touch him without falling
apart.

If she were to put her hands on his naked flesh, no
matter why, all she would want to do would be to wrap
her arms around him and hold on tight, grateful that
he hadn't been seriously injured by that slashing knife
blow.

Her first priority when she returned home was to have
a shower—somehow she just didn't feel clean after her
close contact with Shane.

Luckily she was able to angle the shower-head so
that she didn't soak the dressing on her neck—a hair-
wash would have to wait—but it was wonderful to feel
fresh and clean as she pulled on a pretty, matching
housecoat over her nightdress.

Barbara had been quite right when she'd said that
it was better for her to take the rest of her shift off,
Emma thought; but what she hadn't told her was how
to stop her brain from racing at a hundred and fifty
miles an hour as it endlessly replayed the traumatic
events.

She tried to block out all thoughts of the personal

trauma involved—the shock that her boss hadn't known about, when the two men in Emma's life and heart had suddenly collided inside her head.

There was a knock at the door; Emma uncurled from her position on the sofa cushion and padded silently out of the lamplit room to take the safety chain off and release the catch.

There was no point, this time, in looking carefully through the spyhole—she already knew who was waiting out there.

He was leaning back against the wall opposite her door, one foot crossed over the other and his arms folded across his chest to cradle a small bundle.

He was totally silent and unmoving, his face still and inscrutable as he waited for her to speak.

'Adam.' She stepped to one side as she opened the door wide to allow him to enter. 'Go straight through,' she invited, and closed the door behind him, taking a few seconds to re-secure the chain to give herself time to control her unsteady breathing and the galloping of her heart.

'Coffee?' she offered as she walked on bare feet towards the tiny kitchen. 'I bought some real beans.' She dredged up a smile but it wasn't returned.

'Oh, Emma.' His husky voice broke completely and he was across the room, hauling her into his arms, the bundle he'd been holding so carefully falling to the floor.

'I thought he was going to kill you.' The words

were muffled as he buried his face in her hair and enveloped her so tightly against him that her feet left the floor.

'Adam…' After her initial shock at his uncontrolled reaction she couldn't help her hands coming up to cradle his head against her, her fingers spearing through the lush, straight silk of his hair, until she dislodged the thong that restrained it.

'Adam, are you all right?' She tried to lean away from him, raking her fingers through the thick dark profusion to hold it away from his face as she tried to catch a glimpse of his expression in the subdued light. 'How badly were you hurt? Did you need stitches?'

'You talk too much,' he groaned as he wrapped his arms around her waist until she was hardly able to breathe. 'Just let me hold you. I need to feel you close to me.' And he rocked her in his arms as though she were a child.

Relief.

The sensation poured through her like an uncontrollable avalanche, as though he was unable to restrain it from overflowing, and Emma stiffened reflexively, reminded instantly that there were so many things that they had to talk about.

'Adam.' She pushed against his shoulders with both hands until he finally lowered her feet to the floor and loosened his hold.

She took a couple of steps backwards until his hands dropped away from her and the contact between them was broken. Her head tilting back, she met his darkly gleaming eyes.

'Did you know I was listening to you?' she demanded. 'How long have you known it was me?' In her agitation the construction of her sentences fell apart. 'Were you laughing at me, that I had no idea who you were?'

'No, Emma. No. It wasn't like that.' He ran his own fingers through the heavy fall of his hair, clenching them in its depths as though fighting with frustration.

'At first I had no idea *who* was listening to me. I hadn't expected *anyone* to be able to pick up my thoughts. The last thing I expected when I came over to England was to be able to communicate like that, even though the other person couldn't or wouldn't reply.'

He held his hands out to her in entreaty, pleading, it seemed, for her to understand.

'Then, when I discovered you were sensitive, I put two and two together. The chances of there being two separate people with that ability in the same small area…' He shrugged his broad shoulders as if his conclusion had been inevitable.

Emma shook her head in disbelief. When he put it like that it *did* seem obvious. How could she not have seen it for herself?

'I didn't realise that you and my midnight stranger were the same person until you walked through the door of the emergency room. I was so scared that

Shane would accidentally cut me and panic and no one would find me until it was too late.' All the tormented thoughts of those endless minutes were tumbling out uncontrollably.

'When I heard the voice in my head telling me to hang on I was amazed that he'd been able to hear me, let alone find me.'

'Emma…?' His voice was tormented as he held out both hands to her, his expression full of entreaty.

Slowly she lifted her own shaking hands and reached out until she could place them in his.

Need. Longing. Desperation.

For the first time Emma was unable to tell whose thoughts belonged to whom, because each of them was consumed by the overwhelming relief that the other was safe.

'Oh, Emma…'

Suddenly, as if he could bear it no longer, he swept her into his arms and his lips met hers in a kiss of such overwhelming tenderness that it took her breath away.

'I need you,' he murmured between the kisses he scattered over her face. 'I need to make you mine.' And he took her mouth again, his lips parting hers, his tongue exploring her inner tenderness with an earthy eagerness that made her burn for a deeper possession.

'Adam, please,' she whimpered, her hands longing to explore his body without the barrier of clothing, her fingers plucking at his shirt.

'Ah, Emma, my Emma.' He captured both her hands in his and raised them up to kiss each finger. 'Are you sure?' His dark eyes burned with an inner fire as he gazed into hers. 'Is this just a reaction to the trauma you've been through?'

'Oh, Adam, no.' Emma knew that her heart was in her eyes as she gazed up at him. 'It's because I love you.' And she threaded her fingers through his hair to pull his lips down to meet hers.

The world spun and dipped as he carried her out of the room, finding her bedroom unerringly to lower her feet to the floor beside her bed.

Emma reached out to switch on the bedside light, the golden glow picking out the gleams of light in his eyes and along the dark strands of his hair where they framed his face.

'May I?' he requested formally as he reached for the tie to her housecoat, then slid the soft fabric from her shoulders to drape it over the foot of the bed.

His eyes travelled avidly over her and her pulse rate doubled as she realised that her nightdress must be all but transparent with the light behind it...

'May I?' Emma echoed, stifling her nervousness as she raised shaking fingers to unfasten the buttons of his shirt and pull it away from his body.

'Adam,' she moaned as the narrow, taped dressing was revealed, curving around the base of his ribs. She ran remorseful fingers lightly over it, hating the fact that he'd been hurt.

'It's not important,' he reassured her, shrugging his shoulders out of the shirt and dropping it over her housecoat.

'Oh,' Emma breathed when his torso was revealed in the subdued light. 'You're so beautiful. Like a bronze statue…'

She couldn't resist running her hands over the warm, naked splendour of his muscular shoulders, glorying in the satin smoothness as she stroked her palms down the lean length of his spine in an uncanny replay of her dream.

His leather belt was in the way when she tried to slide her hands inside the waistband of his jeans to find out if the rest of him lived up to her erotic imaginings.

'Help me,' she whispered, trying to unfasten it, fumbling as she manoeuvred the clasp.

'Ah, Emma.' He captured her hands again and brought them up to his lips. For long moments his eyes gazed deep into hers, as though he was making an important decision, then he nodded and drew in a cleansing breath.

'May I give you a gift, Emma? Something from my Blackfoot heritage to mark such a special day?'

Emma nodded, intrigued, as he raised one finger in the air and strode swiftly towards her sitting room, returning almost immediately with the package he'd been holding when he'd arrived.

'This was my mother's.' He held it out to her on

his open palms, his attitude almost reverent. 'After to-night it will belong to you.'

Emma lifted it from his hands and unfolded it, finding the fabric as soft as velvet and more supple than anything she'd ever known.

'It's elk-skin,' he told her as she held it up to reveal the simple shape of the robe. 'Will you wear it for me?'

'Of course.' Emma smiled up at him, knowing that there was a special significance to his request. Later she would ask him to explain. For now, it was enough that he wanted her to wear it for him.

Unembarrassed, she slid her nightdress from her shoulders and he helped to lower the robe over her head.

'Perfect,' he breathed as he turned her to face the mirror and ran his fingers through her hair to spread it out over her breast. 'You see?'

Emma looked in the mirror at her reflection, but all she could see was Adam standing behind her, his eyes fiercely possessive as they watched her, the width of his naked shoulders framing her slenderness, his bronzed arms coming around her to pull her into the shelter of his strength.

'Now, Emma,' he murmured as he leant forward to lay his cheek on the crown of her head. 'Now you will be mine.' And he turned her to face him.

As if she was infinitely precious, he explored her

face, outlining each of her features with gentle finger-
tips, seemingly committing them to memory for ever.

'So delicate...so perfect,' he whispered as he
anointed her with tender kisses, then took her lips with
his own.

Emma had never known anything like the kisses she
shared with Adam; the physical sensation of their lips
meeting, parting and meeting again was intensified by
her sensitivity to his emotional response.

Mine, she heard him say inside her head, while at
the same time her ears heard the soul-deep groan
which emerged from his throat when she opened her
lips to him. *Mine,* she echoed as she began her explo-
rations again, this time mastering his belt and pushing
his last remaining clothes away.

'Ahh,' she breathed softly when, at long last, she
saw him in all his glory. 'I *knew* you would look like
this.' She heard the satisfaction in her own voice as
her eyes travelled over his naked body, her hands totally unable to resist the temptation to explore his lean
hips and cup the tight muscles of his buttocks.

'Dear God,' Adam gasped in a strangled voice.
'When did you learn to drive a man crazy?'

'When someone came into my head at midnight and
taught me to dream,' she whispered just before he bent
his head to ravish her mouth.

'Oh, Adam, it's not fair,' she moaned when he finally released her. 'I'm wearing too many clothes.'
She brushed herself against his aroused body, the soft

elk-skin robe abrading her aroused nipples and sliding over her sensitised skin.

'That's easily solved.' He bent to ease his hands up under the hem of the elk-skin to curve around the sides of her calves. The supple fabric gathered on his wrists as he slid his palms slowly up to her hips and then her waist, his eyes concentrating on each inch of her as it was revealed, his thick dark lashes throwing crescent shadows over his sculpted cheek-bones, hiding his expression.

When he finally drew the robe off over her head her hair was released to drift down around her shoulders and over the pale smoothness of her breasts.

'Like a priceless ivory statue,' he murmured as he put the robe aside, his hands returning to shape and caress her. 'But warm and soft...'

He bent to lift her into his arms, and placed her gently on the cool bed before lying down beside her.

As if in a dream, Emma found herself responding to his every move and thought, her body growing heavy with arousal at the mental images that Adam was sharing with her.

He was patience itself as she took her time exploring his body, and she smiled with delight at his reaction when her nails came into contact with the deeper copper discs of his flat male nipples, tormenting them until they tightened into tiny buds.

Her roving hands travelled further—pale wraiths feathering their way over the earthy reality of his powerful body, until his ragged breathing and the sweat-sheened quiver in his tense muscles told her how much control he was exerting.

'Enough,' he growled when he finally reached his limits and rolled onto his back, pulling her with him so that she straddled his thighs.

'Adam!' she squeaked at the unexpected manoeuvre, steadying herself with a hand on each of his shoulders.

'Sit up,' he urged, propping his own shoulders against the pillows piled at her headboard. 'Sit straight and proud, as you did when you went riding with me.' His hands outlined her shoulders and stroked her arms while his eyes caressed the naked symmetry of her aroused breasts.

She had a mental image of herself and knew that it was coming from Adam's mind as he pictured the two of them in the shadowy light, her skin gleaming like pearl, the light fractured into glimmers in the tumbled profusion of her midnight-dark hair, her eyes shining silver, widely dilated with arousal.

In her mind she saw his image of her cupping her breasts in her hands and leaning towards him to offer them to him like ripe fruits, and found herself powerless to resist.

'Ah, Emma.' Never had his eyes looked so fierce as he accepted her offer, parting his sensuous lips to taste the bounty she was offering.

She hadn't realised the effect his ministrations

would have on her until he suckled her strongly and, for the first time, she felt her womb contract inside her.

'Adam?' The sweet fire was spreading as he continued, his teeth and tongue intensifying the sensations until she was moving rhythmically, unashamedly. 'Adam...I need...I need...'

His hands were caressing her, shaping her, guiding her, but she felt so empty, a great ache building inside that she didn't know how to assuage.

'Ah-h-h...!' Her head dropped back and she groaned aloud as Adam finally filled the emptiness, the ache exploding into ecstasy as he made them one.

CHAPTER NINE

SUNSHINE was pouring in through the window when the alarm finally woke Emma early the next morning, and she lay still for a moment, wondering at the happiness that filled her.

'Adam,' she breathed as the memories flooded through her, and she rolled over under the rumpled duvet to find the bed empty.

For a moment she wondered if she had dreamed the events of the previous night the way she had before, but this time there was more than her aroused body as evidence.

This time she had the tell-tale redness of her nipples to prove that Adam had suckled them into arousal not once but several times in the long, passion-filled night. Her thighs, too, bore the evidence of more than one gallop on her tireless stallion.

She stretched lazily, sensuously, enjoying the lingering sensations in her body that told her she had been brought to ecstasy over and over again, and that her eager body was ready and willing for more of the same.

The night hadn't only been filled with the joys of the flesh.

Long hours had been spent in quiet conversation as they'd each spoken of their lives before they'd met.

Adam had told her of his tribe and the part of Montana where they lived. He'd described Chief Mountain in the northern part of the state and told her of its importance in the spiritual life of his people. He'd explained the significance of the vision quest—a tradition which survived only in a few areas such as his grandfather's—and the journey he'd made as a young man to Chief Mountain.

He'd painted word-pictures which deepened the impact of the mental images, his voice resonant with conviction as he'd described the ritual of the days and nights of fasting and praying.

Finally he'd told her of the dream he'd had of the grey wolf who had become his spiritual guide and mentor and from whom he took his name.

While he'd been speaking, Emma had remembered the strange vision she'd had when she and Adam had sat side by side at the top of the hill the day they'd gone riding together.

She'd forgotten to ask him what he thought it might mean but now it seemed obvious—if he was Adam Grey Wolf, and she had dreamed of a female wolf joining the male, then that could only mean that she was going to be Adam's mate.

'Oh, Adam,' she groaned, and rolled over to bury her face in the pillow which carried the smell of his body. 'I need you here with me…' She wrapped her arms around the pillow but it was a poor substitute.

Pouting with disappointment, she made her way to the shower to start getting ready for work, the thought that she would soon be seeing Adam lending wings to her efforts.

Soon she and Adam—the man she loved, the man she'd given herself to body and soul without reservation—would find a space in their hectic timetables to sit down and make the important decisions which would shape the rest of their lives.

Too excited to stop for breakfast, Emma sped towards St Lawrence's, her brain going over all the reasons why Adam hadn't been able to stay until morning.

She hadn't heard a high-pitched bleep as the hospital called him in for an emergency, but then she'd been so exhausted towards dawn that she doubted whether she'd have heard anything short of a nuclear explosion. She certainly hadn't felt him leaving her arms and her bed, nor heard him dressing and letting himself out of her flat.

She smiled tenderly as she realised that he must have been concerned about her reputation and had made certain that he wouldn't be seen leaving her flat at an embarrassing time.

Still, she consoled herself, there would be other mornings—many other mornings—for them to wake up in each other's arms.

She smiled again as she remembered folding away the elk-skin robe, and wondered what special significance it had carried for Adam. Perhaps he would have time to tell her later today...

'Good morning, Marilyn,' she said cheerfully as she made her usual cursory check of the internal post rack.

The carefully groomed blonde head jerked up from its perusal of a letter and Marilyn's cheeks grew red as she quickly crumpled it in her hands and shoved it out of sight.

On her way to her locker Emma smiled to herself at the thought that even an aggressive vamp like Marilyn had secrets she wanted to keep.

She'd been on duty for half an hour and Adam still hadn't appeared. She didn't want to draw attention to what was happening between the two of them before Adam was ready, but finally she had to ask someone.

'Isn't Dr Wolf on duty?' she asked with what she was afraid was a rather transparent attempt at subtlety.

'He's not here any more,' Marilyn said as she replenished the supplies on a suture tray, her eyes never leaving her task. 'He's gone back to America.'

'He...?' The shock robbed her of breath so that it was several seconds before she could speak. 'When? When did he go?' There was a roaring sound in her ears and she held on tight to the side of the trolley, afraid that she was going to pass out.

'This morning.' Marilyn's reply was blunt, making

it difficult for Emma to ask for details without giving herself away. 'Didn't tell you, did he?' There was a nasty slyness to her tone. 'Never did think you'd manage to land a big fish like that one.'

Emma hardly noticed when Marilyn left the room. Her brain seemed numb and her stomach was cramping as if she was just about to be sick.

Adam had gone. Back to America. Without a word to her. The disjointed thoughts were a mirror of the way her body was moving, her actions more suited to a robot than a human being.

Why? her heart was screaming. How could he, after the night they'd spent together? Hadn't it mean anything to him?

The notification of the imminent arrival of several victims of a car crash was the only thing which managed to switch her brain to automatic pilot. For the rest of her shift she made certain that she was outwardly the same woman she'd always been—friendly, efficient, hardworking.

Only *she* knew that the person inside the familiar shell was mortally wounded, bleeding from a cut that went soul-deep.

Every time she heard a deep voice she went still until her foolish heart realised that it wasn't *his* voice—was unlikely to be *his* voice ever again.

Every time she saw a tall man with broad shoulders and dark hair her pulse doubled until he turned round, but it was never Adam—how could it be when he was half a world away?

For days she waited for a letter to arrive, either at her home address or at the hospital, to explain why he'd had to leave so suddenly. She imagined the words he'd use to tell her when he'd be coming back for her, or the invitation he'd send for her to join him for a new life in America—together.

It never came and hope began to die.

Slowly, over the next few weeks, she learnt that it was so much harder to cover up the emptiness once you had learned what it could contain. Slowly, she began to grow a callus over the wound so that it was less sensitive.

Eventually, she began to harden her heart against the man who'd known better than anyone how fragile her trust was and had still broken it.

She was so grateful that she had a job she enjoyed, a job she could immerse herself in for hours at a time without thinking of the handsome man who'd let her fall in love with him then stolen her heart when he went away.

It was nearly four weeks before the realisation dawned that she wasn't the victim of a lingering stomach bug.

'Adam's baby,' she whispered as she laid a trembling hand over her stomach. The paraphernalia for the home testing kit was staring at her from the side of the basin, the indicator an unequivocal positive.

For several terrified seconds she wondered how on earth she was going to manage to take care of a baby on her own. How was she going to provide for it and bring it up the way a child deserved to be brought up?

The problems were legion but they couldn't outweigh the sheer joy at the prospect of carrying Adam's baby. In spite of her anguish at his betrayal, she was ecstatic she would give birth to his baby and cradle it in her arms.

Was it a boy, with his father's serious eyes and devastating smile? Would he grow up as tall and handsome as his father? Would he too become a healer? Or was it a girl safely nestled in her womb, her features the perfect female counterpoint to her father's masculinity?

It was so long before she would find out and she was already impatient, the secret knowledge putting a shine in her eyes and a spring in her step for the first time since Adam had left.

'You're looking happier,' Dave commented later that day, when Emma was teasing him about his failure to impress one of the new nurses assigned to A and E. 'Has he finally written?' he added softly, after a quick glance around to make sure that no one else was close enough to hear.

'He...?' For a moment Emma was genuinely puzzled. 'Who?'

'Adam Wolf.' Dave frowned. 'I thought it was a

rotten trick to just disappear like that, but if he's been in contact—'

'No!' Emma's face grew pale and clammy as she suddenly realised what he was saying, and she fought to continue in a calmer voice. 'No. I haven't heard from…anyone.' She wouldn't…couldn't say his name aloud. 'What on earth made you think I was waiting for a letter?'

The question was sheer bravado and it didn't fool Dave. He'd known her too long, and in spite of his joking and playboy theatricals, he was a shrewd people-watcher.

'Come on, Em. I saw the way you were when he went back. If I'd been able to get hold of him I'd have—'

'No, Dave. It wasn't his fault. He didn't make any promises and I knew right from the first day that he'd be going back some time.' She shook her head and swallowed to give herself a second to get her voice under control. 'He hasn't written and I'm not expecting to hear from him.'

She'd managed to defuse Dave's anger, but he was still unconvinced by her assurances that she'd just had a nice surprise that morning which had given her a boost.

She went back to work, determined that no one should be able to detect how she was feeling from now on. She hadn't realised that she'd been wearing her heart on her sleeve, and that everyone had guessed what had happened between herself and Adam Wolf. This time she couldn't afford to let anyone guess her secret.

In the quietness of her room she scanned the small pile of publications she'd gathered in her quest for another post. It had taken nearly half a day before the significance of Dave's observations had dawned on her, and she'd suddenly realised that it wouldn't be long before all her colleagues knew that she hadn't just been abandoned by Adam Wolf but that she'd been stupid enough to allow herself to get pregnant.

Ah, but what magnificent stupidity!

The abandoned papers slid unnoticed to the floor in an untidy muddle as she lay back against the pillows and rested both hands over her stomach. A smile softened the lines of tiredness as she visualised the tiny being resting safely inside.

'I don't regret it,' she vowed, hoping the little scrap would be able to sense the truth of her words. 'I don't regret a single minute of it. He was…' There weren't words to describe her memories of what had happened that night, and her voice faded away.

Her thoughts continued, though—and her memories of his gentleness and his passion; the pleasure he'd given her while he'd taken his own had been something she'd never dreamed of in her wildest imaginings.

And out of that overwhelming satisfaction had come

this—her hand stroked slowly over the skin that would soon grow taut round the swollen evidence of their joining.

It was worth it, she told herself as she hugged her secret to herself. It was worth all the heartache and loneliness she'd experience as she pulled up the few fragile roots she'd put down since she'd moved to St Lawrence's.

It was worth moving to somewhere where she knew no one and no one knew her, so that her pregnancy wouldn't be the source of avid gossip and her child would grow up untainted by vicious tongues.

With renewed determination she rolled over and retrieved the pages of advertisements, the most likely ones already ringed in pencil so that she could start sending off her applications.

'It's just the two of us,' she murmured softly into the quiet. 'And we're going to do just fine.'

It took several weeks of writing and waiting, followed by a series of interviews, before she was finally able to hand in her resignation.

'We're very sorry to be losing you,' Barbara Noone said when she was informed of Emma's impending departure. 'I'm only too pleased to give you a reference; you're an excellent worker.'

'Thank you.' Emma smiled with pleasure. 'I'm sorry to be leaving but…' She made a wry expression. She'd explained her reasons to Barbara, knowing that she would understand the necessity. Everyone on the staff would soon be counting on their fingers… 'I haven't told anyone else why I'm going—just that it's a family matter. I've enjoyed working at St Lawrence's and I respect my colleagues too much to want to leave them with lies.'

Nurse Noone's attention was briefly caught by someone waiting outside her door, but whoever it was moved away at that point and she dismissed Emma back to her duties.

There was no let-up in the pace of work, the motorway providing them with plenty of casualties on top of the usual mixture of cases from the circle of towns and villages they served.

Emma was glad to keep busy, her self-reliance coming to the fore again as she determined the new course that her life was going to take.

Her new post was going to be very similar to her present one at St Lawrence's, the Memorial being a large hospital further north, built to cope with the busy region between two major industrial areas.

They'd been delighted to find out that Emma had plenty of experience working on a motorway rescue team, as they'd been hoping to expand their capabilities further in that direction.

One of the older women at her interview had raised a disapproving eyebrow when Emma had informed them of her pregnancy, but, when Emma had pointed out that it was the hospital's generous provision of day care for staff children that had attracted her to apply for the post, she'd appeared mollified.

Emma took the time when she was looking for accommodation to explore a little further out from the hospital, and found the biggest difference between the Memorial and St Lawrence's would be the distance she would have to travel to find a quiet hilltop.

Eventually, with the aid of a large-scale contour map, she found one and toiled her way up in bright sunshine to sit herself at the summit.

It would never be the same as the day she and Adam had sat together but, when their baby was born, she would carry it up and explain the importance of listening for the voice inside him or herself.

Most of the time there would be nothing there and the solitude would only afford a measure of peace and tranquillity, but sometimes, when you least expected it, the voice would be there, loud and clear.

She walked slowly back down, her spirit calmed and strengthened by the time she'd spent there, and resolved that, once she had moved, she was going to haunt the local libraries until she managed to learn all she could about the life of the Blackfoot tribes.

Adam's child might never meet him, but she would make sure that it knew as much as she could find out about the uniqueness of his heritage.

Now it was just a case of moving herself halfway

up the country and getting herself settled in. The rest
of her life she would just have to cope with day by
day.

Apart from the change in regional accents, there was
very little difference in her work when she finally
started at the Memorial.

The staff were the same as she would find in any
hospital in the country, and the patients the same mixture of helpful and obstructive, brave and frightened.

Her first shift started off fairly quietly with a child
cradling a broken arm after a fall off a kitchen stool.

'He wanted to get his own cereal packet down,' his
tearful mother explained as Emma finished wrapping
the plaster bandage around the slender arm, smoothing
it into shape with the palms of her hands.

'I've told him and told him it's not safe to climb
up there…'

'Well—' Emma smiled consolingly '—they do say
boys will be boys. Just think how helpful he'll be
when he's big enough to reach by himself.'

'If he lives that long,' came the wry comment. 'He's
already fallen out of his cot and his high chair. Last
time he tried to climb up on the kitchen stool he
slipped and pulled it over and nearly knocked his teeth
out.'

'Have you thought it might be possible to change
your cupboards around?' Emma suggested. 'If you had
the safe things that he can help himself to on a level

that he can manage, perhaps he wouldn't go mountaineering to find them.'

'There'd never be any food in the house!' she laughed. 'It's obvious you haven't got any young children of your own to deal with…' She was still laughing as she led her son out, the young tough not looking in the least bit chastened by yet another visit to hospital.

Once they'd disappeared round the corner, with a cheeky grin and a wave of the uninjured arm, Emma's answering smile faded. No, she hadn't had any experience with young children, except for the patients she'd met in her job—but she soon would have.

She ran a surreptitious hand over the barely perceptible mound covered by her disposable plastic apron and smiled secretively.

Soon.

She pulled a face as she felt the gypsum drying on her hands, and started to clear up the bowl of milky-looking water. It was a messy job, but luckily it was one she was well-versed in and could do fairly quickly.

Her next patient was an ambulance man who'd been assisting in the transportation of an elderly gentleman who hadn't wanted to go to hospital.

'He'd had a bit much to drink and fallen over. There was blood all over the side of his head, but you'd have thought I was trying to murder the old sod.' The young ambulance man held out his hand for Emma to look at.

'Bugger bit me, right through my glove,' he complained. 'Thank goodness my tetanus shots are all up to date. It's bad enough having to take the antibiotic cover.'

He screwed his face up as Emma gave the wound a good soap-and-water scrub.

'There's no point pulling that face,' she chided. 'You know as well as I do that a human bite is much more dangerous than a dog bite. You wouldn't thank me if I just gave it a delicate dab of povidone-iodine and you ended up with a major infection.'

'You're right,' he groaned. 'Get it over with.' And he distracted himself by asking all sorts of getting-to-know-you questions, his eyes letting her know that he liked what he saw.

Emma glanced at the good-looking blond-haired, blue-eyed man and found herself totally unmoved. It seemed as if there was only one right combination for her, and she was unlikely to find it at the Memorial or even in England.

The more reading she did and the more she thought about it, the more she was coming to realise that she had a certain amount in common with wolves herself.

The book she'd borrowed from the library had painted a picture of wolves as faithful, family-oriented animals who chose mates for life. Unfortunately the mate she'd chosen hadn't felt the same way about her.

There was one decision she had to make that she was putting off until later, although she knew it wasn't going to get any easier. At some stage she was going to have to get in contact with Adam to tell him that he'd fathered a child. Logically, she knew that the chance of his finding out accidentally was infinitesimal and she could have kept the fact to herself for ever, but she couldn't have lived with herself if she'd done that.

Just the thought of writing such a letter was enough to give Emma a bad case of the shakes.

What would he do when he found out?

Would he ignore the letter, believing it was a ploy to bring him back to her? Or would he get a solicitor to reply? Would he acknowledge parentage and then ignore the child's existence from then on, or would he insist that his child had a chance to get to know him?

There were so many possibilities that she could have driven herself mad just contemplating them.

In the end she made her decision; she would wait until the baby arrived so that she could send a photo with a covering letter. That would give her a nice long time to compose the letter and, at the same time, would give her a good reason for delaying making contact with him—a clear case of putting off until another day the things she couldn't face doing today.

Emma went to bed early that night, exhausted by the double strain of familiarising herself with a new place of work and the drain on her body of the rapidly developing foetus inside her.

The tiredness had gradually been accumulating as, night after night, she'd fought to get a good sleep.

Oh, she hadn't been disturbed by intrusive voices; she didn't even seem to have any sensitivity to her patients any more, her gift apparently dormant for some reason. The biggest problem she had at the moment was an ongoing dream about a tall, dark-haired, broad-shouldered man with gleaming black eyes.

No matter how tired she was when she went to bed, the memories were there waiting for her as her head touched the pillow, and she woke each day quivering with arousal, her grey eyes heavy with unshed tears.

'Why don't you get a prescription for some sleeping tablets?' Megan Jameson had suggested when Emma had confessed to sleeping badly.

Emma's first thought had been for her unborn child, but she hadn't been able to say so. There would be time enough for the news to get out. In the meantime, no matter what the books said, she wouldn't be taking anything other than vitamins and minerals while she was pregnant, and then only the ones prescribed by her obstetrician.

'It's probably just getting used to a new bed,' she'd said dismissively. 'Anyway, if I take those things, I'll sleep through my alarm like Rip Van Winkle. I'd do better to go for a walk or take some exercise.'

'If you need to do some exercise before you're tired enough to go to sleep, you're obviously not doing enough work,' one of the charge nurses had called out. 'Give the girl another job to do.'

Emma had laughed with the rest of them, glad that she'd been accepted into the closed world of a hospital so quickly. For all that she didn't talk about herself, she'd begun to make friends and already had a couple of invitations to join groups going out to celebrate birthdays and exam successes.

If only her heart was in it, she thought as she cleared up after a particularly harrowing car accident.

She knew that she was doing her job well—her glowing recommendations from St Lawrence's meant that she would soon be contemplating taking on more responsibility as she continued her climb up the professional ladder.

Unfortunately it felt as if there was some sort of glass wall between herself and the rest of the world— as if her emotions had been put into storage when Adam had left her.

For now, she wasn't worried. Once the baby arrived everything would change. She could feel a deep well of emotion filling up, just waiting for the arrival for it to pour out.

Once the baby arrived…

She fell asleep with her hand resting on the barely perceptible evidence of that new life, a loving smile gentle on her face.

* * *

Loneliness.

Emma sat up with a jerk, her heart pounding as the echoes of an overpowering emotion eddied through her.

Pain.

Before she could block it the emotion slammed into her, almost robbing her of breath. What was happening? Who *was* this overwhelming her in this way? She'd been so sure that these feelings had gone when Adam had returned to America.

Anger.

There was such depth of feeling in the emotion that she felt herself start to shake.

'Stop it!' She speared her fingers through her hair and clutched at her head. 'Don't *do* this to me. I can't bear it…'

The shock of the violence of the emotions, coming on top of her pregnancy-induced tiredness and her broken sleep, was enough to crack her self-control, and she burst into tears.

'Whoever you are, get out of my head…please…' And she sobbed as if her heart was breaking.

It was a long time before she calmed down enough to go back to sleep, her thoughts drawn back to the last time she'd had someone speak to her in the night.

Only one other person had ever reached her so loudly and clearly, and when he'd gone she'd believed that she would never hear anything like it again.

Now there was another one. Someone else with troubles on their mind who wanted someone to share them with. The only problem was that she didn't think she could bear to go through it all over again. It would bring everything back too clearly.

She was still tired when she woke up the next morning, groggy from the lack of sleep and numb from the tears she'd shed.

The bloom she'd heard that pregnant women enjoyed seemed to have passed her by, she thought, catching sight of herself in the mirror as she stripped off for a shower to wake her up properly.

Her hair refused to co-operate as she tried to skewer it into submission. She'd seriously contemplated having it all cut off to get rid of the constant reminder of Adam's delight in it, but when it came to it she'd only been able to allow the hairdresser to trim the ends.

The circles around her eyes were more marked than ever this morning, thanks to her tears in the middle of the night, her face seeming even paler by comparison. No one looking at her without make-up would believe that it was mid-summer. She looked like something that had crawled out from under a dark rock—all wan and etiolated.

'No more,' she muttered with determination. 'I've got to look after myself for the baby's sake...don't I, Little Wolf?' She stroked the smooth, unmarked skin of her belly as she gave the child its nickname, longing for the first time when she would feel movement in there to make it real.

'From now on, we're going to do the right thing all the way down the line,' she said aloud. 'Eat right, sleep right, get lots of fresh air and exercise. You'll be so healthy when you finally arrive…' Her eyes gleamed with determination.

'Last night was just a minor hiccup.' She straightened her shoulders. 'Today is the start of a whole new regimen.'

By the time she was ready for the short walk which would take her to the accident and emergency department at Memorial, she'd had a proper sit-down breakfast instead of her usual coffee and toast held in either hand while she scurried about looking for tights and shoes.

There was a new swing to her stride as she walked swiftly through the maze of streets which took her to the huge complex—part Victorian, part brand-new—that was the Memorial.

Her head was up, her shoulders back and her carriage proud as she murmured with determination, 'This is the first day of the rest of my life.'

CHAPTER TEN

'ATTEMPTED suicide.' The trolley swung past Emma, narrowly missing her on its rapid way into the emergency room, the paramedic reeling off the vital information.

'Female, twenty-four years of age, found surrounded by empty drugs containers. Blood pressure ninety over sixty, pulse a hundred and eight. She was barely conscious when we found her, but she's out for the count now.'

'Do we know what she's taken?' Emma was supervising the patient's transfer off the ambulance trolley, hooking the bag of saline to a stand so that it could flow unobstructed into the IV set up *en route*.

'A cocktail.' There was a rattle as he turned out the contents of a plastic bag. 'We found empty containers of aspirin, codeine and paracetamol, and a number of tablets scattered on the floor by the body.'

'So she's taken two non-narcotic analgesics and one narcotic analgesic all available without prescription and all with a high rating for overdose. Do we know how long ago she took them?'

'Closest estimate is less than two hours ago.'

'So a fair number could still be in the stomach. I'll

set up ready for aspiration of the stomach contents, and then we can administer activated charcoal.'

Gastric lavage was one of Emma's least favourite procedures and she was glad to be called out to another patient partway through, as her own condition seemed to be making her more squeamish than usual.

By the time she'd finished using cyanoacrylate glue on a minor head wound on a child who'd come up underneath a cupboard door, she had her stomach back under control again.

She returned to find the young woman awake and tearful, her face and hair spotted with the dark grey evidence of the charcoal she'd been given.

'Let me get you comfortable,' Emma offered, wiping her with a warm cloth.

'What's the point?' her patient said defeatedly, her voice hoarse from the treatment. 'I'm only going to have to do it all again.'

'Why?' Emma kept her voice gentle. 'What's gone so wrong that you want to do that to yourself?'

'I'm pregnant.' She began to sob. 'I'm pregnant and the father doesn't want to know.'

'Have you told him?' Emma probed.

'He walked out before I could. What am I supposed to do—go running after him?'

'Is he worth running after?'

There was a long pause before she answered.

'Yes,' she whispered.

'Well, then. Don't you think you ought to be deciding which outfit you're going to wear to knock his socks off when you go to tell him?'

There was a watery smile which disappeared as another thought struck her. 'What if he doesn't want it? What if he doesn't want *me*?'

'So what?' Emma made her voice brisk, although the whole conversation was striking far too close to home for her comfort. 'You don't need a man who isn't man enough to face up to his responsibilities, do you? There's plenty more fish in the sea.'

'But what about the baby?'

'Do you want the baby?' Her hand strayed towards her own waist and she linked her fingers together to keep them still.

'I don't know.' The pale blue eyes filled with tears again. 'I don't know how I'd cope.'

'That's one thing about pregnancy,' Emma said wryly. 'It gives you plenty of time to think about things. If you decide you can't keep the baby there are hundreds of people desperate to adopt. There are so many options…'

There was a soft cough behind her and she looked over towards the door to see a policewoman waiting.

'Is it all right for me to do my interview now?' The woman was pleasantly spoken, with a kind expression in her eyes.

'Are you feeling up to it?' Emma turned back to her patient.

'Yes.' It was hesitant but there was a new strength

to the girl's voice. 'It's got to be done so I might as well get it over with.'

Emma was moving away to give the two of them some privacy when the young woman called her back.

'Thank you for talking to me—I feel as if you really understand what I'm going through.'

Emma smiled, her cheeks stiffening with the effort as she thought, If only you knew how well I understand. And she left them to their business.

The conversation kept playing through her mind at odd times during the day. She couldn't help remembering her own voice asking the young woman, Is he worth running after?

She was saddened to realise that, in all the weeks since Adam had left, it was the first time that the thought had occurred to her. She'd asked it of a complete stranger but she'd never thought of applying the criterion to her own situation.

Between dealing with an elderly woman with a strangulated hernia and a house painter who'd fallen off a ladder and had a suspected fractured skull, the answer became obvious. Of course he was worth running after! But, by the time she had contacted the appropriate secretary for an ophthalmic surgeon to see an amateur welder who had somehow managed to get his contact lenses stuck to his eyeballs, she was convinced that she had left it too late.

She was exhausted by the end of her shift. Not just because they'd had several casualties from a gas explosion, who'd needed a great deal of attention before they were stabilised and ready for transferral to the special burns unit, but because of the mental battle she'd been fighting with herself all day.

She stripped off her uniform and pulled on a simple cotton dress, grateful that she'd never been one for dramatic, clinging clothes emphasising her waist. At least her ordinary clothes would last her for some time after her shape began to change.

The cool water felt good as she splashed it over her face and she decided not to bother with make-up. She was only going to walk around the corner to her flat and she was unlikely to see anyone she knew—at least, not anyone that she wanted to impress.

She grabbed her bag, weighed down with copious quantities of fresh fruit and vegetables in accordance with her new resolution, and made her way out of the hospital.

All the way back to her flat she was conscious of a strange sense of impending danger.

She looked over her shoulder a couple of times but there was no one there. She even searched through her other senses to see if she could find anything, but it was as if there were a blanket of cotton wool between herself and the rest of the world.

'It must be because I'm tired,' she muttered as she made her weary way along the last few yards to the main door of the converted house. 'I just need to lock myself behind my own front door and sit down with a hot cup of tea.'

'Taken to talking to yourself, have you?' a deep, accented voice said close to her ear as her bag was lifted out of her hand. 'Why don't you invite me in? I think I deserve a little of your conversation.' And he took hold of her elbow to hasten her steps inside the house.

'A-Adam!' For a moment she thought her knees weren't going to hold her up, and she swayed precariously as joy flooded through her.

'Keep walking,' he growled, 'or I might be forced to carry you. It's taken me long enough to find you, so you're not getting any chance to disappear until I get some answers.'

Suddenly she realised that Adam was angry—no, more than angry, furious.

Her confusion was so great that she didn't even think of arguing with him about his high-handed tactics, meekly allowing him to usher her through the tiny communal hall and into her flat.

He followed her closely across the room until she sank gratefully into a chair and kicked off her shoes; then, when she expected him to sit in the matching chair, he leant forward to grasp an arm of her chair in each powerful hand and loom over her menacingly.

'Why did you do it?' he demanded, his voice low and bitter. 'You could have told me.'

'Do what? Told you what?' Her head was twisted

at an awkward angle as she tried to look up at him. She couldn't think straight while he was hanging ominously over her like a great dark thundercloud.

'Don't try to play the innocent.' There was disgust in his voice too. 'The blonde nurse told me—Marion Something, the man-eater.'

Emma allowed herself a wry grin at the thought of Marilyn's reaction to hearing Adam's description of her, but she was no closer to knowing what he was talking about. What on earth had the stupid woman been saying?

'I couldn't believe it at first.' He straightened up and turned to pace away from her, his long legs covering the tiny space between her and the chair on the other side of the room far too soon. 'So I went to Barbara Noone and she confirmed it.'

'What?' Emma's frustration boiled over. '*What* did Marilyn tell you? *What* did Barbara Noone confirm?'

'That you left St Lawrence's because you were pregnant with my baby.'

Emma was stunned. How on earth had *Marilyn* found out, of all people? She was certain that Barbara Noone wouldn't have told her...unless... A memory surfaced. Had Marilyn been the shadowy figure outside Barbara's office when Emma had been telling her...?

'Is it true?' he demanded hoarsely, his hands clenched tightly into fists. 'Did you leave because you were pregnant?'

'Yes,' she whispered, knowing that this had been the last way she had anticipated breaking the news to him.

His shoulders slumped as though he'd been struck a mortal blow, and he sat down as though he'd lost all strength.

'Why did you do it?'

Suddenly she was able to feel the pain coming off him in waves, and she realised that until this moment he'd somehow been keeping a tight control on his emotions so that she couldn't read them the way she had before.

'Why did you kill it? I would have taken it if you'd told me—'

'What?' The word emerged as a startled squeak. 'What did you say?'

'It's not the first time,' he said, almost too quietly for her to decipher the words. 'Jaqui got rid of my baby before I knew she was pregnant. Said she didn't want a half-breed brat even if its dad *was* going to be a doctor able to earn a good living.'

The pain was years old but was still festering deep inside.

'Adam.' Emma took a deep breath and stood up, walking towards him on shaky legs. 'Please, give me your hand.'

She held out her own hand and waited, almost counting the beats of her racing heart as she willed him to comply.

Slowly he raised his head to look at her, his face drawn taut with torment, and she could feel his confusion.

She met his gaze fearlessly but couldn't manage the smile he needed for encouragement, so she settled for patience.

At long last she watched his knuckles regain their normal colour as he released his hold on the arm of his chair.

'Feel,' she whispered softly, her throat too tight for proper speech as she directed his palm over the slight roundness hidden by her dress.

Emma? She watched him form the word soundlessly as happiness filled his eyes like the sunrise after a long dark night. 'The baby's still there. Couldn't you go through with it?'

'I never had any intention of getting rid of it—that's why I moved.'

'But…?'

'If I'd wanted an abortion I could have had one without going through all the upheaval of changing jobs and moving,' she pointed out. 'St Lawrence's is less than an hour from several private clinics on that side of London. Anyway,' she challenged, 'what on earth made you think I wanted to have an abortion?'

'Your friend Marion.'

'Marilyn's *no* friend of mine,' Emma stressed. 'She's a self-centred bitch on the lookout for a wealthy husband.'

'But when I stopped off to leave the letter she said she'd make sure you got it...' His words died away as he saw her shaking her head. 'You didn't get the letter?'

A brief flash of memory reminded Emma of Marilyn's blush when she had caught her reading a letter which the girl had rapidly hidden.

'Not only did I not get the letter but I suspect my "good friend" opened it and read it.' She wrapped her arms around herself as the feeling of betrayal stole over her.

'Oh, God, Emma, I'm sorry.' He surged to his feet and took her in his arms, pulling her close until she rested against the warm security of his body, with her head tucked under his chin.

'I left early that morning so you wouldn't be the object of gossip, fully intending to set the record straight as soon as possible. Unfortunately, when I got to my place there was a message that my grandfather had been taken ill and I had to go straight away.'

'Oh, Adam. Is he all right?'

'He will be. He's too stubborn to die yet.'

'What was the matter with him?' the nurse in Emma couldn't resist asking.

'A heart attack. He's needed bypass surgery for some time, but kept refusing to have it done.'

'Why did he agree this time?'

'Because I told him about meeting you.' Adam's gaze was very intent. 'I told him about your gift and

your incredible way with people, and I told him about
the mental rapport between us and that I wanted you
to marry me and bear our children.'

'If you told him all that, why didn't you tell me?'
The words were a cry from the heart. 'I woke up in
the morning after the most incredible night of my life
and you'd gone.' She drew in a deep breath and held
it, fighting for control.

'I wrote it in the letter,' he said simply. 'It was the
first love letter I've ever written in my life and you
never saw it.' He wrapped his arms tighter around her
and rested his cheek on her hair. 'I said thank you for
the most wonderful night of my life. I told you that
my grandfather was ill or I'd never have contemplated
leaving you like that. I wrote my address and telephone number so that you could contact me and said
I would be coming back for you as soon as I could.
And I said I love you…'

He cupped her chin with one lean hand and tilted
her face up to his, his eyes gleaming gold in the soft
evening light. 'I love you, Emma Sullivan. You're the
other half of my soul. Will you marry me?' And he
lowered his head to brush his lips over hers in the
tenderest of benedictions.

'Oh, Adam, I love you too.' Her hands slid over his
shoulders to cradle the back of his head, her fingers
dispensing with the leather thong so that his hair
spilled over his shoulders as she pulled him towards
her to deepen the kiss.

Within seconds the fire was blazing out of control as the weeks of loneliness were swept away by passion.

Clothing landed in haphazard piles on the floor between the sitting room and her bed, until finally they were once again naked in each other's arms.

This time they knew how to arouse each other swiftly enough for the sparks to fly. This time they made love with an urgency that bordered on compulsion, as though the time they'd spent apart had left them starving for each other.

I love you.

The overwhelming emotion needed no words as they reached ecstacy together, their minds and bodies in perfect harmony.

'I'm sorry I couldn't come back any sooner.' Adam's voice was husky as he ran his fingers through her hair, spreading it out in an ebony curtain across the pillow.

'Once I'd got my grandfather to agree to the operation I had to stay until he was well on the way to recovery.'

'What did he say when you told him about me?' Emma was curious.

Adam laughed. 'He said it would be worth giving up the principles of a lifetime to be treated by Western medicine if it meant staying around long enough to meet the wolf's mate.' He cupped her cheek and turned her to face him. 'You are, you know.' His voice was serious. 'You're Grey Wolf's mate, and he mates for life.' The words were as binding as if they'd been spoken in front of a priest, and he lowered his head to seal the vow with a kiss.

It was a long time later before they spoke coherently again, but Emma had questions that needed answers.

'Where will we be living, Adam?' Her question was a tacit agreement that she would go wherever he wanted.

'I…I've decided that I can do most good if I return to Montana,' he said slowly. 'Some areas are heavily populated and the facilities are as good as anything you're used to, but some are far more remote and primitive and the people there have so little…'

He'd been lying on his back with one hand under his head, the other arm cradling her shoulders as she cuddled close to his side. He rolled over towards her until they were facing each other.

'Will you be disappointed that we're not going to Seattle? You would have been much sought after for your ER skills.'

'Emergency Room?' she guessed.

'Yes.' He smiled. 'You're almost bilingual already.'

She thought about the experience she could gain in one of Seattle's big hospitals, but the prospect paled against what Adam was offering.

'I'd rather be where you grew up,' she said quietly. 'I want our child to see the things you saw, learn the things you were taught.' Suddenly she remembered the vision she'd seen and told him about it.

'I was thinking about my visit to Chief Mountain when we were sitting on the hill, and I saw the female join the grey wolf too.'

'That was one reason why I was so upset when you went away,' Emma told him, and she knew that he could feel her pain. 'I knew I was falling in love with you and thought the vision meant that we were going to be together, especially when you told me about your vision quest.'

While she was speaking Adam's eyes were caught by something on the bedside cabinet, and he reached across to pick up a small pile of books.

'*Wolves*? *The First Americans*? *The Indians of the Plains*?' He read each title questioningly.

'I wanted to know about your people and your background so I'd be able to tell our child.' She rested her hand over the slight curve and he placed his reverently beside hers.

'Now you won't have to read books about us; you're going to be one of us and my grandfather can tell you what you want to know.'

'Does he know about the elk-skin robe?' Emma remembered the ceremony with which he'd given it to her. 'You said it was special but I haven't found anything about it in these books.'

'It's part of an old Blackfoot legend which tells of the grandson of the sun god being given an elk-skin robe. It was to be worn only by a virtuous woman who, once a year, would honour him in the sun dance so that the sick might be restored to health.'

Emma felt her cheeks grow warm at the implied compliment, her love growing for this special man with every hour she knew him.

Contentment.

They smiled at each other, marvelling at the difference a few hours could make in the course of a life.

'Do you think our children will inherit the gift too?' Emma's voice was growing sleepy.

'More than likely.' Adam's words had a husky undertone as he stroked her naked body, exploring the subtle differences her pregnancy had already made.

His fingers teased the pale globes of her breasts and she arched her back, her reaction telling him better than words that they were now even more sensitive to his ministrations.

'Ah-h-h, Adam, yes…' The sleepiness was disappearing fast as he began to make love to her slowly and thoroughly.

'I've been thinking, we shall have to do this often in the next six months,' he whispered against her rapidly tightening nipples, his hands already parting her thighs for his exploration. 'If our children do inherit the gift from both sides of their family, there's no telling when we'll be certain we can make love without having eavesdroppers…'

Emma laughed delightedly, the sound filling all the

dark corners in the room. 'If ever I heard of finding a good reason for doing exactly what you wanted to do in the first place...' She smoothed her palms over his back to urge him closer, then grasped the tight curves of his buttocks explicitly.

'Far be it from me to deny my mate...' he murmured, and as they became one their simultaneous 'I love you' rang out loud and clear in the soft light.

The first few faint streaks of colour were lighting the early-morning sky when Emma opened her eyes, and her hand slid across the rumpled bedclothes to find an empty space.

There was a lingering trace of warmth which told her that Adam hadn't been gone very long, and she slipped her arms into the shirt he'd worn the day before to go to look for him on silent feet.

Their ranch-style house had more windows than walls, as befitted its location in a place of almost unlimited views. As soon as she'd seen it, Emma had understood Adam's long-ago comment about the horizon being so close in England. Here it seemed as if you could travel for ever before you ran out of space.

She came around the corner into the long, open-plan lounge and found another view of the sunrise, the colours growing stronger and brighter by the minute.

Silhouetted against the light was the familiar, beloved outline of her husband as he stood gazing out on his world. As she watched he bent his head and she realised that he held something in his arms—or rather someone.

Good morning.

She smiled as he communicated with her in a way that seemed totally natural now, neither of them needing to voice their joy in each other, neither needing to look to know when the other was near.

'Emma.' He turned partway towards her and held out one arm to welcome her at his side.

'What are the two of you doing up so early?' she chided. 'Weren't your beds warm and comfortable enough?'

Adam smiled in that familiar heart-stopping way.

'We were going to come back in a minute but I had to show him to the sun.' They both looked down at the tiny replica of the tall man holding him and saw that his dark eyes were fixed on the brightness outside the window.

'Don't you mean, show him the sun?' Emma smiled as she stroked the petal-soft skin of the baby's cheek with the tip of one finger.

'No. I'm following an old family tradition. When each new baby is born we show him to the sun and give thanks for the gift we've been given.' His arm tightened around her shoulders and he lowered his head to brush a gentle kiss over her lips.

'In fact—' he brushed his lips over the downy dark hair crowning his son's head '—I feel as if I should be here every day giving thanks for what I have—for what *we* have.'

Emma couldn't help agreeing. They lived in one of the most beautiful places on earth, doing jobs they loved, and they had found in each other the perfect other half. Now, with the birth of their son, already nicknamed Little Wolf, everything was perfect.

Without needing to say another word she wrapped her arms around her two men and gave herself up to a feeling of total contentment.

I love you...

I love you, my love.

For the rest of their lives the message would be loud and clear.

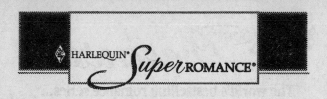
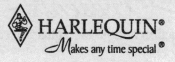

HARLEQUIN *Presents*

**The world's bestselling romance series...
The series that brings you your favorite authors,
month after month:**

Helen Bianchin...Emma Darcy
Lynne Graham...Penny Jordan
Miranda Lee...Sandra Marton
Anne Mather...Carole Mortimer
Susan Napier...Michelle Reid

and many more uniquely talented authors!

Wealthy, powerful, gorgeous men...
Women who have feelings just like your own...
The stories you love, set in exotic, glamorous locations...

HARLEQUIN *Presents*

Seduction and passion guaranteed!

HARLEQUIN®
INTRIGUE

WE'LL LEAVE YOU BREATHLESS!

If you've been looking for thrilling tales of
contemporary passion and sensuous love stories
with taut, edge-of-the-seat suspense—then
you'll love Harlequin Intrigue!

Every month, you'll meet four new heroes
who are guaranteed to make your spine tingle
and your pulse pound. With them you'll enter
into the exciting world of Harlequin Intrigue—
where your life is on the line
and so is your heart!

THAT'S INTRIGUE—
ROMANTIC SUSPENSE
AT ITS BEST!

HARLEQUIN®
Makes any time special ®

Harlequin® Historical

From rugged lawmen and valiant knights to defiant heiresses and spirited frontierswomen, Harlequin Historicals will capture your imagination with their dramatic scope, passion and adventure.

Harlequin Historicals . . . they're too good to miss!